NEIL CAMPBELL

ZERO HOURS

CROMER

PUBLISHED BY SALT PUBLISHING 2018

2 4 6 8 10 9 7 5 3 1

First published in Great Britain in 2018 by
Salt Publishing Ltd
12 Norwich Road, Cromer, Norfolk NR27 0AX United Kingdom

www.saltpublishing.com

Salt Publishing Limited Reg. No. 5293401

A CIP catalogue record for this book is available from the British Library

ISBN 978 1 78463 148 2 (Paperback edition)
ISBN 978 1 78463 149 9 (Electronic edition)

Typeset in Neacademia by Salt Publishing

Printed and bound in Great Britain by Clays Ltd, St Ives plc

Salt Publishing Limited is committed to responsible forest management. This book is made from Forest Stewardship Council™ certified paper.

For John G Hall, Manchester poet

PART ONE

I WALKED IN on my first shift and was met by the manager, Hakan. He was a little prick. I could see it from the start.

'What time do you call this?'

'Eh?'

'You should be here, ready to start at the beginning of your shift. Don't come late. Where are your gloves?'

'Oh, I forgot.'

'You forgot? Are you dense or something?'

'I'm not dense. I forgot.'

'Go and get the gloves and then come and find me.'

I went for the gloves as he walked the other new starters to the conveyor belt. All around me there were men pushing metal trolleys. The ceiling lights were dull and left faint shadows. There was red movement all around: the Royal Mail uniform for permanent staff. When I came back I was put on tipping, which meant I wheeled a trolley full of sacks to the end of a conveyor belt and tipped each sack of post out onto it. After about an hour I could feel my dodgy knee beginning to ache. My back was aching too. Every time I looked up from sacks or the conveyor I could see Hakan's eyes peering back at me. A bit later he brought a load of people over to watch me working.

'You see? This is what I'm talking about. You have to work more quickly.'

He walked over, brushing me out of the way, and then picked up two sacks at once, tipping them all onto the conveyor.

'You see how much quicker that was?' he said, to the new starters, who nodded.

I'd seen this kind of shit before. Yes, he could do that once, but try doing it hour after hour. I knew I had to pace myself. I was on minimum wage. When Hakan went I carried on as I was. He looked back at me later in the shift and kept shaking his head. I threw an A4 Jiffy bag onto the conveyor. It felt like it had a hardback book in it. I would have liked to have rammed that Jiffy bag in his face. I carried on dropping parcels onto the conveyor. There was an Asian woman on there, throwing the mail into the baskets. She was about five foot tall.

Hakan came over and told me to go onto the conveyor. I did, and stood there throwing first class mail, second class mail and airmail into the right baskets. When those baskets were filled, someone came and wheeled them to the other side of the warehouse.

At the end of the night we walked in processions, pushing the trolleys out onto the loading bay where other workers wheeled them up ramps and onto the back of the lorries. Round and round we went, one following the other, shoving the full trolleys then wheeling back the empty ones.

Zlata was pushing an empty trolley back. She wore a bright yellow T-shirt and was tall and slim and blonde.

'All right?' I said.

'All right,' she said, mocking my Mancunian accent.

'Are you the only woman working here?'

'YES!'

'I'm a writer.'

'Writer? Woo hoo!' she said, and with that she was gone, pushing the empty trolley through the depot.

For the rest of that shift I saw her in flashes of yellow. She flung parcels into baskets, worked hard.

There were two breaks of seven and a half minutes each. On the second break, I wandered into one of the brightly lit canteens that dotted the perimeter of the depot. Zlata was there, leaning back, glugging from a big bottle of water.

'Can I sit here?'

'Okay.'

'Thirsty?'

'Don't be an idiot. So . . . you are a writer? Very good, Mr Writer. So, Mr Writer, what do you write?'

'Poems and short stories mainly. I've got a novel.'

'A novel? Fantastic. What is it about?'

'Being a writer.'

'Ha! That sounds *so* boring.'

'It is what it is. So . . . is this your dream then . . . working here?'

'I have a postgraduate diploma in international relations, from Salford University.'

'I used to work there. You know the Clifford Whitworth Library?'

'Oh, I was in there my whole life!'

'So, are you finding that qualification useful?'

'What?'

'International Relations?'

'Of course! All nationalities here.'

'How long have you been here?'

'Almost one year.'

'So, you're permanent?'

'Yes. After three months, they give you more money.'

'Not sure I want to be permanent.'

'It is good job.'

'I've done worse.'

'In this economy it is not easy to get jobs.'

'I know.'

'Anyway break time is over,' she said, standing up and pulling her T-shirt down over her midriff.

'Shall we go for a drink after work?' I asked.

'Okay, why not? I give you chance. Wait for me outside, Mr Writer.'

Hakan told me to go on skips. Skips was an area of waist-high baskets filled with mail. Standing there I got talking to this fat bloke. I could smell beer on him.

'That Hakan's a tosser,' I said.

'Tell me about it.'

'Every time I looked up he was there, staring over.'

'They're all cunts in here, mate, all the management. Bunch of cunts.'

As he spoke, he kept flinging post from the waist-high basket into any one of a semi-circle of bigger baskets, labelled with postal codes. Half of them were tiny yellow Jiffy bags. He threw them with a flick of the wrist and they floated into the baskets every time. Mine were going all over the place.

'Cunts in this place, I tell you. Watch your back with that Hakan. Can't say anything to him. Say anything to him and everyone will know about it. Little blokes are always like that. Like Yorkshire terriers, vicious little bastards. The way he talks to me . . . sometimes I'd like to rip his head off . . .'

'Yeah.'

'He's a total fuckface.'

'I get the picture. So . . . you local then?'

'Just round the corner, just up there,' he said, pointing. 'Collyhurst.'

'I'm in Didsbury.'

'Didsbury eh? The leafy suburbs.'
'Yep.'
'That's the posh part of Manchester.'
'I'm not from there though. I'm from Audenshaw.'
'Oh yeah? I know it there. Used to have a mate in Denton.'
'Oh, right?'
'Yeah, he was an arsehole.'
'Cheers.'
'No, I don't mean that, I mean Hakan. Tosser he is. I tell you, one of these days I'm going to ask him what his postcode is and then I'm going to throw the little bastard into a basket.'
'I'll watch my back.'
'I would.'
'Anyway, it's nearly ten. Are you doing the night shift?'
'Nah.'
'They'll come round in a minute asking if you want to do nightshift.'
'Fuck that.'
'Don't blame you. But I need the dough. My bird has got the dolly blue and she's been off.'

At the end of the shift I stood outside, waiting for Zlata. A car sped down Oldham Road, headlights tracing the tarmac. Two lads in T-shirts and caps stood outside the takeaway, across the road, smoking. There was a queue at the bus stop, several guys still in their high-vis vests or red Royal Mail shirts. I watched through the glass doors as Zlata chatted to several lads. Eventually she came out.
'Everyone wants to take me for a drink!'
'Doesn't surprise me.'
She started swinging her bag around in the air.

'Where are you taking me?'

'You know Gulliver's?'

'No.'

'They've done it up. Used to be a dump.'

'A dump?'

'Yeah.'

'I don't come out for drinks with people from work. Hardly ever. Okay, well, sometimes. Maybe once per week. Twice per week sometimes. Ha ha!'

In the pub, we sat opposite each other on high seats. There was a table between us that meant I couldn't see her body. Behind the bar, the mirrors sparkled.

'So where are you from?'

'Sarajevo.'

'Oh right.'

'Bosnia. You know in Bosnia I was a reporter there. Quite famous.'

'Really?'

'Yes. Political reporter in Sarajevo.'

'So why are you working in the mail centre?'

'It is complicated. I'm not English.'

'You must miss it.'

'I miss my mum. And my sister. I miss them so much.'

'I can imagine.'

'We never forget the siege of Sarajevo. You remember?'

'I'm shit on politics.'

'You don't know? Oh, my god.'

'Sorry.'

'Siege was for years. I was a teenager. Coming here, work in mail centre, you think is hard work? That is ridiculous. Nothing is hard for me now. We come here and your people say go back to your own country, don't take our jobs. English people don't do the jobs we do. Have you tried to live in a war? And what is your problem here? Brexit? You vote Brexit? You are stupid in this country.'

'I didn't vote for Brexit.'

'The snipers were the worst. They were in tower blocks, they killed women and children. How is that for conscience? They even shot at us in the cemeteries.'

'I don't know anything about politics, like I said. Look, there is a poetry night on across the road, why don't we go there? It will be a laugh.'

'That is your attitude? I give you my heart and that is your attitude? Drink your beer and watch your football because that is all you English know.'

'We are going to poetry, aren't we? I'm listening to you, aren't I?'

'You don't listen. How can you understand? Here is no problem. You think England is so special? The weather here is so awful, and the food, oh my god. And the people are not kind.'

'Well, why did you come here then?'

'That is all you can say? You are not sensitive. How can you be writer when you have no political conscience?'

'More to life than politics.'

'You are so stupid.'

'No I'm not. I just don't know about Bosnia, sorry.'

'You don't know anything. You are not writer.'

I walked her back to the bus stop. She got on the 81 and didn't look from the window as I waited. I stood in the shadow of a Ferris wheel, the so-called 'Wheel of Manchester'. There was some dispute about the rent and it wasn't going around.

I wrote in the morning and had a kip in the afternoon before getting on the bus for the long trip back across town. It seemed like everyone else was heading home. Bright sunlight glinted from windows. The CIS Insurance building rose high into the sky and shimmered in the haze. A group of men on Oldham Road stood topless, washing cars in the heat.

Temporary staff didn't get lockers at the mail centre. So I went to the cloak room. There was a broken tumble dryer covered in dust. A single table with chairs around it. There were no coat hangers or hooks and the chairs had layers of coats on them. Rucksacks and bags littered the floor around the table. I kept my valuables in the pockets of my jeans. I went out to the conveyor, remembering my gloves. Hakan was holding some high-vis bibs.

'I see any of you without the high-vis on you will be fucked off out of the door.'

He pointed towards the trolleys and I went back on tipping. I could see Zlata. Every time she threw a letter into a trolley she bent forward across the table. I wrote a poem about it that would eventually find a home in a short-lived journal produced by undergraduates at a university in the middle of nowhere.

The writing was going okay. I had a short story in a prominent anthology. It was reviewed by a critic, famous in academic circles. I had two of his books. He didn't understand Sherwood Anderson either. This critic was now reviewing stories on his own blog and hadn't had anything in print for a while.

I'd stopped going to readings. At the last one I'd been to, the friends of the writer who made up the audience laughed uproariously at his sly irony and clapped and whooped at the end. If they didn't already know him the jokes wouldn't have been funny.

I also went to an experimental poetry night at the Castle, across the road from Gulliver's. The first act was a bloke with a beard sat at a desk, typing into an Apple Mac while orchestral music played. He was typing the notes to the music. After that, someone else came on and passed bits of paper around to the audience. To great amusement, we were all asked to write a line of poetry. After that, the poet collected the bits of paper together, smiled to herself and walked off. There was tumultuous applause. Then it was time for a richly deserved break. I got out of there.

I went to another reading at the Burgess Centre where this writer had just read from a new book. It was a collection of short stories made to look like a novel. He was so smug, talking with his editor. There was a Q&A. The prose in the book, for all its attention to minute detail, was utterly boring. The detail said nothing except that the writer was a good observer of banality. But he had the last laugh. I fell for it and bought one.

Back in the mail centre, I got talking to this bloke from Bolton. He had a heavy beer gut and wore glasses.

'How long you been here then?'

'Thirty-five years,' he said, pushing one of the trolleys into place and almost barging past me to get another one.

'I bet you pay more in tax than I'm getting paid,' I said, as a joke.

'Get hold of one of them,' he said, pointing to a trolley. 'Wheel it over there.'

I wheeled one of the full trolleys of post over to where all the other ones were, waiting to be taken out to the lorries at the end of the shift. I repeated this over and over. I paced myself and thought of other things. Poems, potential stories, stories I was already working on.

The bloke from Bolton had sweat pouring from his head as he marched with one trolley after another to the loading bay. I kept strolling, even when he stared.

'Have you been ticking them off?'

'Eh?'

'You're supposed to tick them off every time.'

I followed him over to a little desk at the side of the conveyor belt. There was a white board on it and little lines written in marker pen, counting off the trolleys taken to the loading bay.

'Tick that every time. Fuck's sake.'

I'd seen him going to the desk but nobody had told me to tick anything. I looked over and he was talking to Hakan and pointing at me.

Hakan came over. 'Are you ticking them off? Make sure you tick them off. You should be doing six of them every thirty minutes. I will be watching. Six.'

I didn't speed up. Fuck that. The Bolton bloke chipped in again.

'You're a bit slow you, aren't you?'

'Not piece work, is it?'

'No, I mean, you're a bit stupid, aren't you?'

'Don't call me stupid.'

'Well you are, aren't you?'

'Are you winding me up?'

'Ha ha! Got you there, you dick!'

We carried on, the sounds of the depot all around: strangulated shouting, trolleys being wheeled, engines, occasional forced laughter. There was a radio on somewhere. Sixties melodies drowned out by noise. A rising high note. The Bee Gees. A middle-aged woman came around with a plastic bag of sweets. I took one of them. She did it every night. The Bolton bloke watched me as I unwrapped a Werther's Original.

As I worked I saw two men staring at Zlata's tight jeans. One man said something to the other, and they both laughed.

'You know, I have written a poem about you,' I said to Zlata, at break time.

'Oh yes?'

'It is about your arse.'

'Ha. What a surprise.'

'I know. I'm going to stop doing that.'

'What?'

'Objectifying women.'

'Good!'

'Can we go for another drink?'

'I don't know.'

'I'll wait for you outside.'

After break the bloke from Bolton was back again. 'You ticking them off?'

'Yes, I'm ticking them off.'

'Sure you're a bit dense.'

I pushed my trolley into his, knocking him back. His eyes widened. 'Don't talk to me like that, dickhead,' I said.

I kept my eye on him for the rest of the shift, but he didn't do anything except work his bollocks off. It was a pride thing. The old con. I'd seen it so often. Poor man had been doing it for thirty-five years and he couldn't see the lie any more. I come along, stroll around. I could see it would wind him up.

I waited for Zlata at the end of the shift, watching as she

fended off her admirers. She came through the glass doors, smiled when she saw me there, swung her bag around in the air, began dancing.

'We are free! We are free!'

'Yep. So, where we going?'

'We go to the pub! The English pub!'

We went in The Castle this time. Like Gulliver's across the road, it had been done up. We went and sat in one of the back rooms, on comfy leather seats.

'You drive those men crazy in there. I see them all looking at your arse.'

'I know.'

'How does it make you feel?'

'How do you think? I hate it. People don't understand.'

'I don't think I did before.'

'Anyway, I have permanent contract now.'

'I know.'

'You can get one. Maybe after twelve weeks.'

'Twelve weeks.'

'Will be better then. Very busy. Lots of shifts.'

'Great. Are you coming back to mine?'

'Oh come on.'

'What?'

'You can wait with me at the bus stop.'

We kissed in the doorway of the old Nobles amusements arcade on the corner of Oldham Street and Market Street. She stopped suddenly and stared at me. Her bus arrived and she ran for it.

It was pretty random, the way they allocated the shifts, and after that night I didn't work with Zlata for ages. I missed her and she didn't get in touch. When I looked at her timeline on Facebook I could see she was forever flirting with men, ending messages with love hearts and kisses so often that those symbols became meaningless. I bet she kissed everyone. One time she put some pictures of herself with another man. Someone called Ryan. They were in a hotel bedroom in Chester. She had her arms around him. In another she wore pearls and a plunging lace neckline.

I put her out of my mind and worked on my writing. I had a story in the *Best British Short Stories* for a third time, but nobody noticed. I kept on with poems, blurting them out in Bukowski-like torrents across reams and reams of notepads. I had no care for form, it was emotion that mattered, that and capturing something. Life was too short for counting syllables. When I realised that syllables didn't really matter in haiku because the 5, 7, 5 thing comes from Japanese anyway, I wrote reams and reams of those too. I immersed myself in Basho, Buson, Issa and Shiki, all the famous ones.

Jack Kerouac wrote them too. Called them 'Kerouac Pops'. Three lines of poetry, simple as. *The windmills of Oklahoma blow in all directions, the winter fly in the medicine cabinet has died of old age.* Something like that. Loved that shit. I had a lovely Everyman edition of haiku too, a little hardback. I carried it everywhere and read it on the bus.

There wasn't much call for haiku at the mail centre. But if I stopped working for long enough, I could see them all around me. *High-vis vests/baskets filled with letters/the mail centre.* Or, *in the loading bay/the drivers chart their route/by sat nav.* Or, *under the safety sign/old woman cold and sweating/among the parcels.*

It was a few months later when I noticed something about

Zlata. It wasn't obvious because I only ever saw her wearing a high-vis vest. But there was a noticeable swell to her belly.

'Why you looking at my stomach?' she said.

'Sorry.'

'I'm off after eleven weeks anyway.'

'What?'

'I go on maternity after eleven weeks.'

'So . . . oh right. I didn't know.'

'I post every day on Facebook! Everybody knows!'

'I didn't.'

'I put about it on my Facebook loads of times.'

'Oh right. I stopped looking.'

'It is Ryan's.'

'Ryan?'

'He is on night shift now.'

'Don't know him.'

'You wouldn't. I was seeing him for a bit. Not now though.'

'Really? What about the baby?'

'He has four other children.'

'He will be involved though?'

'I don't know. It doesn't matter. I'm happy anyway.'

'I didn't know.'

'My parents have said they will help me look after the baby. Maybe I will go back to Bosnia.'

'What is its name?'

'*His* name?'

'Yes.'

'Luka.'

'Right . . . so what was I then?'

'What?'

'So, we kiss and then that's it?'

'Oh, you are so sweet! That was just for fun.'

'Right.'

Break time was over. I watched her walk away and went back on to the conveyor. I flung mail, wheeled trolleys at speed, didn't talk to anyone. Hakan looked pleasantly surprised at my work rate. I worked like that for a bit, mindlessly, counting the days down until weekend.

Then Zlata began messaging me via Facebook. Telling me all the time about what an arsehole Ryan was. How she was going to make him pay child support. How he needed to start every morning with vodka. Vodka she bought for him. I had a look at his Facebook page. It was full of topless pictures. He wore big gold chains and clearly worked out. There were loads of pictures of him with different women. Despite the gym-toned body he looked like he was nearing forty. The women looked older than that.

Zlata told me how great the sex was with him. Another time that he couldn't always get it up. I didn't want to know. She also told me about all the men she'd known. The one guy she loved. She seemed to idolise him. Then there were the guys who beat her. How she was raped. How she'd had nightmares all her life. How she'd had to leave Bosnia. How she had a master's degree and was throwing mail because if you were foreign that was as good a job as you could get. How she worked harder than everyone else. How she worked hard while pregnant. How she believed in the virtue of working hard.

On her last day in work, Zlata didn't do anything except open presents and cards from the people she worked alongside in the mail centre. I knew she'd been worried about people taking the piss. Everyone knew about Ryan. But it turned out Ryan was on long-term sick leave now, dealing with stress, and everyone saw that he was a child, really. As she opened the presents Zlata seemed happy, and I looked at the other workers in the mail centre, saw they weren't so bad.

The mail centre wasn't the same after she left. There were no women for a start, just sweating, belligerent men. Men who'd learned from an early age to mask whatever sensitivity they had behind a front of macho bullshit.

It was the temporary staff who did the bulk of the work in that place. Managers did nothing at all except walk around with clipboards telling people what to do. But there were other people I saw as I pushed trolleys around. Old guys with their feet up on desks reading newspapers or doing crosswords. Other people strolling around handing out gloves or high-vis bibs or sweets. Maybe after so many years the job got better, you were given easier tasks, and looked on as the new staff did all the graft you'd already put in. But then there were the others, like the bloke from Bolton, pulling his tripe out every shift and pissed off if you weren't doing the same.

I was moved around the mail centre at random intervals, Hakan whistling and pointing at me like I was a dog. One night I got chatting to a bloke from Heaton Moor. He'd been moved to Oldham Road after they closed down the depot in Stockport. His name was Kev.

'You were at City?' he said, tossing a Jiffy bag into a basket.

'Yeah. Just as a kid,' I replied, looking at the postcode on a Jiffy bag. There were hundreds of these tiny Jiffy bags, all the same. Some freebie being sent out by a company. God knows. I threw one in a basket. All these baskets had the place names written on, and you had to remember the postcodes.

'So what happened there?'

'Got injured. Did my knee in.'

'Cruciate?'

'Yep.'

'I play five-a-side twice a week.'

'Oh yeah?'

'Stockport Powerleague. You should come down.'

'Not played for years.'

'Don't worry about it. It's just a laugh. Well, some of them are pretty competitive but it keeps you fit.'

'I do miss it.'

'Well, look, give me your number and I will give you a bell if we're short.'

'Whereabouts in Stockport are you?'

'Heaton Moor.'

'Oh right.'

'Near the Elizabethan, you know it?'

'Yeah, think so, had a pint in there once. Guy from the Stone Roses lives round there.'

'Yeah. Mani, or Reni, whatever his name is. We go in the Plough. Anyway, I will give you a bell.'

As I threw the Jiffy bags into baskets, I thought of some of the goals I'd scored at Platt Lane. A lot of people at the mail centre wore headphones. Some people never stopped talking. A lot of people just worked in silence, and I wondered how they occupied their minds.

The five-a-side place was in Heaton Norris. I had a vague memory of having played there as a kid. But they'd changed the AstroTurf since then. Last time I'd played it was really hard, like at Platt Lane, and the ball was always bouncing over head-high. I'd played at Oldham too. Boundary Park. You couldn't tackle on those pitches. It took the skin off your knees. In the adrenaline of the game it didn't hurt, but you'd be picking scabs off for weeks. This new Astro turf was softer, much more like grass.

I started the game slowly, but then began to make little darting runs. I sprayed passes around with both feet, got stuck into hard tackles. After about ten minutes I was on the ground, almost puking. Kev was laughing and told me to go in net. The ball went past me before I got the gloves on.

I got my breath back and when someone else was knackered they went in goal. I couldn't keep running up and down so just went up front. I'd always been able to score goals. When the first one went in I felt like jumping in the air. Under those dull floodlights, in a game played by men with beer bellies, there was still that thrill of scoring a goal. That sight of the ball rippling the net. That lovely rattle of the netting. The cheers and half-hearted clapping of your team-mates. I felt I could keep going if I kept scoring. And if I kept scoring they didn't pull their faces at me for being lazy. I scored four or five goals. We lost 10-8. The best goal was one where I toe-poked it through the keeper's legs. That night I lay in bed thinking about my goals. The image of the ball hitting the netting. I pictured it over and over. In the morning I could barely walk.

Would I still be playing in this City team, chasing Champions League glory? There had been loads of promising youngsters come and go, a lad called Michael Johnson was one I remember. He had it all, and ended up running pubs and bars in Chorlton and West Didsbury. But even he wouldn't have got in the City team these days. Who would I have played for? Maybe I wouldn't have been that great after all. Perhaps I'd have been good in Scotland. Anyone can play in that league.

I played whenever Kevin called me. I changed my game

a bit, didn't really tackle or try to sprint. I put my foot on the ball, passed it about, found space. There was a player at Liverpool once, back in the 80s. Jan Molby, Norwegian bloke. Fat as fuck but a genius. Just stood there, passing it around.

'What do you think about this Brexit thing?' I said to Kev, one night in the mail centre.

'About time.'

'Why?'

'Can't go on like this, can it?'

'What?'

'All these foreigners.'

'Not done City any harm.'

'Ah well, no, of course, we love the Saudis!'

'Could have all gone wrong that.'

'Oh, I know. Shinawatra and all that. Frank Sinatra or whatever they called him. Dodgy fucker. The gods were kind! But you know we can't just let everyone in.'

'We don't.'

'City don't even have any English players. Agüero, Argentina. Silva, Spain. De Bruyne, Belgium, Touré, Ivory Coast.'

'That Touré is a lazy bastard.'

'He's probably the best midfielder we've ever had. Apart from Silva.'

'Come on. He can't even run.'

'What about the goals he's scored in semi-finals, finals?'

'Didn't get his birthday cake, did he?'

'Twenty goals that second time we won the league.'

'He's a lazy bastard. Does my head in.'

'Are you saying that because he's black?'

'Oh, fuck off, will you?'

'Racists if you ask me. All these City fans who have a pop at Yaya. No loyalty any more.'

'I thought we were on about Brexit anyway?'

'Oh aye.'

'Gordon Brown I blame. He let them all in. We need to close the borders. And Brexit, Farage and them, they are the only people speaking for the common man. Farage, you could have a pint with him. He's just a normal bloke.'

'Farage is a racist arsehole.'

'Don't spit the dummy, mate.'

'I'm not.'

'Where's your argument then?'

'He's a racist arsehole. End of.'

'Okay then, mate. You've got no argument. Soft-arse.'

'Look, if your country was being bombed, if you had a famine, if you were getting raped, would you just stay there? With your family?'

'They're taking our jobs.'

'If I hear that one more time I'm going to scream. You're a racist.'

'Look I've got friends—'

'Oh, for fuck's sake. They have to get in open boats, risk drowning, hide in the back of lorries, get frozen to death. How desperate do you want someone to be?'

'Lorry drivers lose their jobs for that shit.'

'Is that all you can say?'

'It's true.'

'You're an arsehole.'

'You're out of order.'

'Oh, fuck off.'

'Don't think you'll be playing football with us lot again.'

'So what?'

'You weren't that good anyway.'

'Whatever.'

'Bet all that City stuff is bollocks. Where's your proof?'

'Oh fuck off, you fat fuck.'

'You fuck off. And when the votes are in, don't come crying to me.'

'Cheesedick,' I said. Then I saw Hakan raising his eyebrows. He was from Turkey. But that had nothing to do with it. He was just a cunt.

I'd been reading *The Grapes of Wrath*. Poor people, starving, forced off land they thought was theirs, forced to move somewhere else in order to survive. And when they get there, they are met with hostility, people who don't want them there, people who can only see their own poverty and not the poverty of others, people looking after number one. I knew loads of good people who voted for Brexit, and Kev was one of them. You couldn't say anything to change their minds.

Those working class that voted for Brexit, and the Tories for that matter, would soon realise that it wasn't foreigners taking our jobs, there were no decent jobs and never had been. Try doing some of this zero hours shit. If you're off sick then drag your arse in because you won't be getting sick pay, you've got no rights whatsoever. Day after day you phone in, asking for work. Day after day you sign in at the desk, just another face from the agency. On the phone, they used to call you for work. Now you have to call them. Time after time it's engaged. There are hundreds of you wanting the work, it's all you can get. The bloke on the phone is exhausted. If you're lucky he will remember your voice. Helps if your voice is English. Once you've started, if you turn up on time and work properly and don't get in any problems then he might even call you. And that call will come an hour before your shift, so you better be ready beforehand just in case, and you'll rush out for the bus across town, keeping an eye on your watch the whole journey. And you'll get off in Piccadilly and almost have to break into a run, down Oldham Street, along Oldham Road, where Royal Mail workers finishing their shift will be passing you the other way, their red jackets flapping in the wind as they head into town for buses home. And the tall glass buildings continue to rise around you, nothing to do with you, and they knock down old brick pubs, all that history reduced to rubble, and the new buildings rise, and the Beetham Tower whistles in the wind, noise-polluting forgotten places like Hulme, and you'll see men, sorting through the rubble, fishing out the undamaged bricks to fling into skips and sell in bits and bats, the old memories of Manchester fading.

In work, I'm daydreaming. I walk across the paddy fields, beyond the saplings that became huge trees, those saplings tied to their support posts by black leather straps. Those posts in certain places are useful as goals. I am on there with Houghy and Brownie, in the summer holidays. Brownie slides through dog shit and it goes up the back of his leg. He wipes it off with grass and dock leaves and we practise overhead kicks. Then we play goomer. I volley one in, and then put a header wide so I have to go in goal. Brownie chips one across to Houghy who volleys it. It flashes past me and into the net. But there is no net. I run for the ball and bring it back. We carry on until dark.

When I was a young boy the paddy fields were also known as 'the tip'. Half of it was landfill, but not like you think of it now. It wasn't piles of plastic with dozens of gulls screeching in the sky above it. It was just a place where people dumped stuff, before there was such a thing as recycling, when nobody had even heard of the ozone layer. The other half was always fields, from the allotments right around to the primary school.

There were slabs of concrete with rusty prongs coming out of them, and the concrete was piled like a bomb site. Me and Houghy climbed into these ready-made dens and once we could have been trapped as the concrete began sliding. Bags of sand and rubble sat there, too heavy to move, and the rain poured on them and seemed to make them heavier, and the bags sagged and sank a little into the ground.

This lad Arnie was older than us, and I didn't see him building it, but I ran over one afternoon to see that a kind of wigwam or tepee had been made out of tree branches. It still seems a miracle to me how he did it. He made a fire in the middle, the smoke rising up and going out through a hole he'd left in the roof. A gang of us sat around the fire playing a game called 'True, Dare, Kiss, Command or Promise'. I was too shy and always left before the game started. Houghy stayed. I remember the light of the fire licking up those green walls, and the idea that Arnie had gone to all that work just so they could play that game.

Once, as a kid, me and Houghy tore a tree apart with our bare hands. We cracked limbs, ripped off the bark, swung off branches and pulled down on those branches like monkeys. There was nobody around to stop us, and so we carried on with our wanton destruction, wrecking until the sun went down and we were knackered, traipsing home over the green railway bridge. I saw that tree the following day. It was all sad and drooping and damaged. I was saddened too at the sight of it. White scars stood out vividly on the broken limbs, the ripped bark flapping.

Some of the piles of landfill rubbish were overtaken by nature over the years, so that they became little green hills. All of the rubbish was populated by pecking birds, and the sour air was filled with their singing and calling. There were dozens of magpies. They seemed to boss the place. When they had young ones, it was a mass of black and white and squawking, and when the sun shone on them you could see all the other colours too, the blues and greens mixed in with the black. The gulls I was less keen on, with their shitting and general insistence. But the crows were beauties, my favourites. The nice contrast of their blackness as they flew past the tip and across the green expanse of the paddy fields.

Nowadays the trees of the paddy fields are so tall they cast long shadows onto where the tip used to be, and the tree I injured is one of the tallest, though maybe if I looked closely, with someone who knows more about trees, I could still find the scars I inflicted with Houghy. Houghy, who died after sniffing glue on the cricket pitch.

One night on my way home down Old Lansdowne Road in West Didsbury I saw a tortoise, heading slowly but surely towards the edge of the kerb. I bent down and picked him up, at which point he disappeared beneath his shell. I wasn't sure what to do so I took him home and put him in a cardboard box. I watched him racing up and down from one end of the box to the other, trying to climb out. He left a big shit in the box. I closed the lid, leaving room for air, and then I went out knocking on doors.

There were posters all over the place for cats. There was

one for a cat with a missing tail, but usually they were the pretty, fluffy ones that went missing. I knew someone who lost her pretty cat. He went missing for months, and she went out every night calling for him. Eventually Pushkin was found, skinny, dirty, scared, but it was a nice story, how they had found each other again. But who owned a tortoise? I didn't know anyone. Barely spoke to the neighbours in my own building save to tell them to turn their music down. When I knocked on the doors of big houses and asked if they had lost a tortoise they looked at me like I was insane.

I looked online. You just fed them salad. They were worth a few quid if you flogged them. He was a Hermann tortoise. I found a website called the Tortoise Protection Group. I even phoned a world-weary bloke on the missing tortoise hotline and reported it to him, registering the tortoise as missing. The bloke was very helpful, but nobody came forward.

I decided to keep the tortoise and call him Hermann. I got him a new box. Gave him the necessary food. After that he stopped scrabbling from one end of the box to the other. I let him out to walk around the flat. Despite the fact that he shat everywhere we were getting on well. He loved it when I stroked him on the head. Then one day I put him back in his box and he didn't come out for two and half months.

I put that box inside another box and put straw in there too. I kept my flat warmer, mainly for the tortoise. I read they could freeze to death if you left them outside. He would have frozen to death in the council flat I'd lived in years before. I had no heating in there for two years. He would never have survived escaping around there either. Someone would have thrown him against a wall or run over him. Most likely they would have sold him. There were times I wish I'd done that.

I thought of that book by Huysmans where he puts jewels on the tortoise. Blings the little fucker. I didn't do that. I just waited for him to wake up.

I was watching a DVD featuring highlights from City's title-winning season the year before when Hermann got up. I rubbed him on the head the way he liked it. The poor sod was groggy as fuck. I shone a torch on him and sat him near the radiator. It was probably the wrong thing to do, and he seemed grumpy, but eventually he began moving about.

He'd always had a little hole in his shell. Didn't seem to bother him. But in summer I had an idea. I got a long piece of string and threaded it through the hole. At the back of the flats there was a little garden that nobody used, though a gardener came now and then to keep it in trim. I let myself in and tied the string around the pole of an old washing line. Then I let Hermann stroll free. He absolutely loved it. He munched so much plant life you barely needed the gardener. I got some more string. Tied it onto the end of the other string. There was a little pond in there and a cracked greenhouse filled with spiders. Hermann loved it. He shat all over the garden. I left him in there all summer. Sometimes I sat out there in an old deckchair I found near the gas meters in the cellar. You could hear the sound of tennis balls from the Albert Club. Sometimes tennis balls came flying over and I flung them back. Hermann was perky as fuck all summer. He needed those two and a half months to kip it off. I loved him, but I needed a woman.

I got talking to Debbie in Didsbury library. She was a little older than me and worked for Siemens on Princess Parkway. She'd been divorced quite a while. Had two grown-up kids.

The lad had just left to go to uni in Bristol and Debbie was upset. She had this daft dog. A poodle.

One night she invited me back to her house on Elm Road. She'd been making us mojitos, and Toby was locked in the kitchen.

'He's going to be lonely in there all alone,' she said.

'Sod him.'

'You can't say that.'

'He's a dog.'

'Yes, and a lot of people, like me, get very attached to their dogs. A dog will never let you down. Men will always let you down but dogs never will.'

'They are animals.'

'Men? Yes, I know.'

'Come here,' I said, pulling her on top of me. She stripped off her top and I buried my head in her cleavage. The dog began to whine in the kitchen and Debbie stopped dead.

'Oh, I can't leave him alone.'

'Fuck the dog.'

'Don't say that!'

She climbed off and went into the kitchen. I heard talking in a childish voice. Finally, she came back in with a couple more mojitos, and the dog came in behind her, barking on and off for a good fifteen minutes before sitting down on the couch between me and Debbie.

We left the mutt in the living room and went upstairs. The bed was against the wall. There were books piled everywhere. Various dressing gowns hanging from the back of the door. We got into bed, cuddled together our naked bodies. I felt myself hardening against her hot skin and climbed on top. She lay there, spread-eagled in the moonlight that slipped between the curtains. I put my hands either side of her and then I heard a growl.

'Oh, for fuck's sake,' I said.

'Doesn't matter,' she said. 'Come on.'

I carried on. Entered her softly, slid in gently. Ignored the dog's barking. I picked up speed. The dog began barking louder. The quicker I went the louder he barked. Debbie began screaming; she was a screamer. The dog barked even louder still. There was a right fucking racket going on in there.

All she'd had to do was put the dog out of the bedroom. If she'd done that I might have put up with him. But she wouldn't. She said he couldn't sleep on his own or else he would be barking all night. She said he'd howl like a wolf if we locked him in the kitchen. So, I jacked it in. I hated that dog. I walked past them both one day, a month or two after. They were heading down to the Mersey for a walk. She was smiling and the dog seemed smug.

I'd get on a roll with women, see two or three in a row before another drought set in. It was a confidence thing. I went with one and I thought I could have them all. Soon I hooked up with a woman via Facebook. We'd worked in a bookshop together, years before. We met up at a lovely big pub in town, The Bank. She came in, tottering on high heels. She was drinking vodka and Coke. I tried one of the single malts. After a few drinks, she got up from opposite and sat beside me, our thighs touching.

'I always did like you,' she said.

'Bit late for that.'

'Why a bit late?'

I pointed out the ring on her finger.

'Oh, forget about that. Look, the little shit has been

cheating on me for years,' she said, putting a hand high up on my thigh.

'But—'

'Hello? What's this?' she said, rubbing my trousers.

'We can't do it in here.'

'Nobody can see.'

We were in the corner, to the right of the bar. But I wasn't about to unzip.

'But you're married.'

'Look . . . I told you, he has been cheating on me for years.'

She kept her hand where it was, moved her face closer. She stank of fags. She'd been going out about every twenty minutes for one all night. I moved to kiss her anyway.

'Not in here,' she said.

I walked her back to the train station. The next weekend she sent me a message on Facebook that she was booking a hotel for us.

'I've got a kid. He's autistic,' she said, taking off her clothes in the hotel room.

'Okay.'

'But you don't need to know about that. You need to know about these.' And with that she walked over to me and shoved her bra in my face.

'What do you think of them?' she said, flopping her breasts out and squashing them into my cheeks.

'Not bad,' I said.

She rode me in a desperate way. Sucked me off frantically so I had to tell her to slow down. I went down on her in return.

'I like my happy endings,' she said, after.

'Good.'

'You don't say much do you?'

'Like what?'

'Doesn't matter. Shall I book it next week?'

'Won't he realise?'

'Doesn't matter.'

When she was in the bathroom I tied a knot in the johnnies and put them in the bin, wrapped in paper towels. She got back in bed. Her arse was tremendous, great wobbling expanses of it.

As she came back from the bathroom I could see she had been crying. I had no idea what to say.

'We shouldn't have done that,' she said. 'I feel really bad now.'

'You said he's a shithead.'

'I didn't,' she laughed. 'Little shit.'

'Same thing.'

We walked out onto the landing. I looked at the wooden banisters on the ornate stairwells. We went down in the lift and called a cab using the phone in reception.

She messaged me again the following week. Same time, same place. The hotel was a shithole, really, but she was paying so I couldn't complain. I bought the drinks in The Bank.

'Having Andrew has been really hard,' she said, later, as we lay in the hotel bed. I sensed she'd been crying again.

'You can't prepare for it. You know what he does now? He just throws things at you. I mean, I love him to bits and I wouldn't change it for the world, but it's hard.'

'I can imagine.'

'I'm not being funny, but you really can't. Nobody can. Unless it happens to you. But the thing is that he takes up all our time. And we get help. It is exhausting. And at the end of the day you've got nothing left. I don't really blame him for cheating on me. I wasn't there for him. He wasn't there for me. He is just so angry all the time these days. And he drinks. He never used to drink. And it changes him. He never used to be so angry. And I'm sure it's changed me too. It's hard. So, I need something that's just for me. And you give me my happy endings. And I just want that for me. Is that so bad?'

'No. I don't think so.'

She started kissing me again.

The next week when she messaged I said not to book the hotel. A few days later she asked me if I'd changed my mind. I hadn't. An hour or two later she asked me what she was going to do now. I told her to go on Tinder and she told me to fuck off.

I met Sam at a poetry night in Whalley Range. She read some funny poems. I asked her if she wanted to come back to mine and she did. Soon as we got in she said it was likely to be a 'one night thing'. She whipped off her top, and the rest came off soon after. I went down on her. She was shaved. Then when she sat on top of me I came pretty quickly. Afterwards I felt too tired to go again. She was young and gorgeous, but everything she did felt like an act. There was no feeling to it. She got what she wanted and that was that. She told me I was number forty-five.

I met Tracy on the same night as she read with some shit-hot poet of the underclass from Yorkshire – a female Joey Ramone drinking pints of Tetley bitter. They were both great. There weren't enough working class women out there reading about their experiences. The literature scene in Manchester was a dick-swinging contest. Tracy had invited me to read at the night she organised in Bolton, and said I could stay over at her house. But she was disappointed with the way I read, I could tell. I wasn't a performance poet, I just read the words.

It was a slam, where judges voted for the best poem and the winner got twenty quid. A big Scouser turned up with his mate, was all shy, said he'd never read a poem in public before. When he got on stage he read an ordinary poem with masses of confidence, and won the £20. On his way out, he and his mate sang, 'Championees, championees.'

I went back to Tracy's terraced house after. Inside there were bikes, toys, crayon drawings with scribbled writing underneath. She made us both a cup of tea and we sat with them in the living room, me on the couch, her on the armchair.

'Good night,' I said.

'Yeah, guess so, love.'

'How did I read?'

'I'm tired, love.'

'You read well.'

'Oh thank you, yes. I wasn't sure about the ones I read but you know the thing is to always start and end with your best ones and so that's what I did and I think they went over okay and it was a good night yes and maybe performance poetry is not your thing I mean like you said it is more about getting published for you. I've got this guy is desperate to publish me but I keep putting him off but I've got an album coming out you know spoken word that will be better. They publish good poets that will be good on iTunes and that and iPlayer or whatever you call it these days anyway I'm daft me I will show you to your room, unless you want to watch some telly, no probably not, you can kip in my bed tonight and I will kip in one of the kids' rooms come on.'

I finished my tea and she took the empty cups into the

kitchen. We walked to the top of the stairs and she pointed to where I was sleeping. 'Night,' she said.

In the morning, we sat in her living room. The blinds were closed. Privacy from the street and the houses across the road. I couldn't think of anything to say.

She said she'd walk me to the train station. It was bright and sunny. She wore tight jeans and a short jacket. When she walked in front of me I said, 'You've got a great arse.'

'Thank you,' she said.

'You don't mind me saying that?'

'No. You are right. I *have* got a great arse.'

'Some women don't like compliments.'

'They need to lighten up, love.'

'You're not bothered then?'

'Obviously it can go creepy, but you're right. I have got a great arse. And in twenty years I won't have. And nobody will say I have. So, I will accept it from you, love.'

We reached the train station and she pointed me to the right platform and said goodbye. She looked happy, walking away in the sunlight.

There was a poem of Tracy's on the train station wall. It was good. It was about the 9 to 5. It's still there. I sat there in the sunlight, waiting for the train. On the way back, I wrote poems about Tracy, one after another, words flowing. But they weren't any good.

The bloke from Bolton was continually winding me up at work. He would bang his trolley into mine, and make jokes about me to other workers, pointing in my direction and laughing. One night I was doing some tipping when the conveyor broke down. The red lights flashed and the work came to a stop. The little Asian woman took the chance to rest. She leaned on the conveyor and closed her eyes. I went over to her and had a chat. Her name was Bal. She seemed surprised that I was talking to her.

I was leaning on the conveyor next to Bal, waiting as Hakan phoned someone to come and fix it, when the bloke from Bolton slammed his trolley into mine.

'What the fuck are you doing?' I shouted.

'What the fuck am I doing, I'm working! You want to try it sometime!'

'It's broke, dickhead!'

'Well do something else. Move a trolley. Go over there and help them lot out over there.'

'You aren't the boss.'

'Look, Hakan would tell you the same. You're a lazy cunt, everyone knows it. And I've had enough.'

'Get off my back.'

'Long as you're here I am going to be here.'

'Oh, get fucked, you Bolton bastard.'

'That's fighting talk.'

'Oh, fuck off.'

'Watch your back. That's all I'm saying. Watch your back.'

'Yeah right.'

'Okay, okay, back to work, back to work!' said Hakan, as the conveyor began its slow turn once again. Bal tried to keep up with the backlog, piles of mail spilling off the conveyor so she had to bend over and pick them up. I slowed down to give her a chance to catch up. Took my time with the tipping. And Hakan pulled his face.

Another lad went on tipping and I moved over to the conveyor. Massive packages came rolling along. Hedge cutters or garden shears, something like that. They weighed a ton and I launched one after another into the second-class basket. I saw how Bal struggled on the other conveyor. The parcels were almost as big as she was.

You were supposed to look at every package to check the postage on it, but if there were loads that looked the same you just launched them all into the same basket. It was the only way to keep up. Anyone with half a brain doing the tipping would take their time, make it easier for you, and you'd return the favour.

I went on my break when Hakan shouted at me to do so. I sat in the canteen area. Bal was chatting happily on her phone. I got up to fill a little paper cup with water from the cooler. There was no water left. I put the empty cup on top of the cooler. The kitchen was closed as it was the evening shift. There was a big dining area, just for the day shift. I went to the vending machine and bought myself a chocolate bar, a bag of crisps and a can of Coke. I sat there at a table, a bright white table in a bright white room. There were posters on the wall advertising outings, again aimed at the day shift. I looked at the shutter doors of the café, closed my eyes briefly, listened to the different languages being spoken around me. There was a TV screen high in the corner. Everyone kept looking up at the screen. I went to the cloakroom. A man in the corner was kneeling on a prayer mat.

I had another book coming out and I got invited to read at a monthly spoken word night. It was held at The Castle, on Oldham Street, just a few hundred yards from the mail centre.

The room was tiny, just half a dozen rows of chairs leading to a makeshift stage. At the back of the room, where they did the sound, there was a little corner bar. The compere, a genial bloke and ambitious writer, introduced the acts. First up was a woman who ran another night at the Three Minute Theatre. She read her poems about cycling around Manchester and all the misogyny she faced. Then there was another woman on the open mic, mate of the compere. She read for a few minutes. The microphone packed up on her but she said she was a trained actress, projected her voice and her poems were great.

They fixed the mic and I read fine, felt confident in my work. People laughed and applauded and were enthusiastic. We sold a load of the books and I signed them for people at the end. It felt good and made me want to keep writing. It was the best reading I'd ever done, pretty much the only good one.

I'd been going to another spoken word night at Fuel in Withington. Sometimes they got a few people in to watch. It was usually just a hardcore of about six or seven poets, all male, mostly middle aged. They were all good, all published, and when other people didn't turn up it was like a really good writing group. And afterwards we all got pissed.

One night a young woman turned up on her own. Sheepskin jacket, long blonde hair, black boots, scarf. She looked like something out of 70s California. She came back from the bar with a bottle of white wine and a handful of glasses she passed around. She was called Anne. She sang her own songs in a rasping voice with her own lyrics some of which were great. Afterwards she suggested heading into town for another drink. I was up for it, and this bloke called Melvin came along too.

The karaoke bar was always a good place to go to if you wanted a late drink. Above the shabby entrance there was the brickwork of a beautiful old building. We walked in down the steps, past the tall black bouncer in his woolly hat and leather coat. There was a folded copy of the *Metro* in one of his pockets. The bar had mirrors on the walls to make it look bigger. The drinks came in plastic glasses. The stage was to the right of the DJ. The lyrics appeared in gaudy font on a widescreen TV on the wall. An old man with a white carrier bag in his hand started singing 'Fairytale of New York'.

One side of the room was cordoned off and there were no other empty seats so the three of us stood by the bar. I looked around. There was another old man. He was sitting alone and doing a crossword in the paper with the kind of pen you get in betting shops. It was quiet at the bar so the barmaid had a chance to sing. But her eyes were dead and she killed the love song. There were three young lads in baseball caps with pints of lager on the table before them. They were all leaning back in their seats, legs apart, the tongues of their trainers lolling out. All three of them were staring at Anne when she left to meet up with her dealer.

When Anne had walked into Fuel earlier in the evening, I couldn't keep my eyes off her. When she got onto the tiny stage with her acoustic guitar, I'd feared the worst. But when she sang it just added to her charm. She had the smoky rasp of a woman in her forties, but, as she told me later, she was only twenty-six.

When she returned to the karaoke bar with the coke in her bag she went straight to the bathroom and came back smiling. When it was her turn to sing, I watched her with the same awed expression as everyone else in that little karaoke bar tucked away on Charlotte Street, just around the corner from Chinatown. Her sheepskin jacket was sliding off the bar, just above her handbag on the floor. I stopped it falling. Anne wore tight stonewashed jeans and a tight black sweater and it was not hard to see why she had a job at Long Legs. She sang Bob Dylan's 'Subterranean Homesick Blues' and the audience cheered their approval. Later, when she got up to sing another tune, there was hardly any applause and the three lads were pretending to ignore her.

Melvin and Anne went to the bogs at various times. I didn't see that much difference in them when they got back. It seemed the coke was just something that helped them stay awake. It amused me, the way people whispered about drugs, like naughty children. Melvin sang a John Lennon tune, 'Mother'. As he did so, Anne turned towards me.

'Aren't you singing?'

'Nah, I can't. I'm happy to watch you. You've got a great voice.'

'I could be famous in a month if I got the right chance. It just needs someone to spot you. I'm doing a music course. I know all about the industry.'

'Is the work you're doing paying for the course?' I asked, noticing a pimple on her left cheek.

'No. That's just paying for how I live!'

'Right.'

'I'm not going to be there long. I've got a five-year plan.'

'Good.'

'Five years and I'll be out of there.'

'I knew a girl worked in Long Legs once. It's like she said, your body doesn't last forever.'

'That's exactly right!'

I noticed a tattoo on the inside of her left wrist, but couldn't make out what it was. On the front of the same hand there was a blotch like a little red cloud. I took a sip from the Jack Daniel's and ice in the little plastic glass. The ice was melting and the glass seemed to be filling. Each time I looked across at the three lads they turned from staring at Anne to stare at me.

'Working there, though,' she carried on, 'I know exactly what men are like and why relationships work. Men and women. We are totally different, as people. When I'm doing the escort work I can see they love their wives. Some of the sad ones tell me and cry. But they get a new fuck and then they go back to their wives. A guy even told me once that he needed to wear a plastic device to keep his erections down. Poor sod. A man can't be faithful. For a woman that kind of thing is psychological. For a man it is just biological.'

'I don't think it is that simple. I think I have to at least like a woman if I'm going to sleep with her. It is psychological for me too. We're not all like that.'

'Ha ha! You think I've not heard that before? You're all the same, course you are!'

'You seem to be dealing with it, though?'

'Well . . . I do a lot of crying when I'm on my own.'

'Really? Why?'

'Well, it's because I lie to my mum about the way I live. Every time I see her. And she is a lovely person. Anyway, I'm going to the bathroom, look after my coat.'

I nodded and watched as she walked away. I looked around and couldn't see Melvin. A skinny middle-aged man in a shiny grey suit was singing Frank Sinatra. He pulled it off with class.

Anne came back, and I really was at a loss to know what she was doing, in a dive bar with two men she hardly even knew. Then I guessed it was so she could have the night out she wanted. She wanted to sing and dance and take coke. And that was it. Having two men around kept predators off.

'I like my girls though. The girls I work with. I like them. They tell me their stories. I try to help them out with money. Not everyone gets the escort work. But you know, I haven't been abused.'

'Why do you say that?'

'Well, that's the cliché about the sex industry, isn't it?'

'I didn't know that.'

'Well I haven't been.'

I was going to ask Anne if she wanted to share a taxi when the bar closed. But the singing went on. I could barely keep my eyes open. I almost wished I'd tried some of the coke. And then Melvin came back, and whispered something into Anne's ear.

'I think I might go soon,' I said, to Anne.

'Oh. Okay.'

'I was thinking we could share a cab.'

'I'm going into the gay village after this, meeting up with some friends.'

'I don't fancy that.'

'Well, like I said, I'm staying out.'

'I've got this urge to look after you.'

'There's at least two things I could say to that,' she said.

'Okay then, look, I think I'm going to head off. I'm knackered.'

'Okay. I'll come out with you. I'm going for a smoke.'

We went up the stairs and out of the karaoke bar. There was a thin coating of snow on the pavements and wisps of it drifting in the air. Anne wasn't even wearing a coat. She held the unlit cigarette and a lighter in the same thin fingers.

She opened out her arms and hugged me. I held her tight and patted her on the back.

'It's been a great night!' she said.

'Yeah. You look after yourself. How are you going to get home?'

'Don't worry! The night is young!'

'Okay, I'll see you then.'

'Might see you at the open mic!'

'Yeah, sure. Look after yourself.'

I walked the short distance to the taxi rank outside the Britannia Hotel. I got in a cab and as it passed the karaoke bar I looked through the window at Anne. She was laughing and smiling and talking with the three lads in baseball caps. I never saw her again.

By now I'd been with the same publisher for ten years. A lovely husband and wife team who made my books look really good and put them out there. He was a poet. Pretty good. Underrated. That they had no money for publicity wasn't their fault. When my first book came out and just disappeared I think I blamed them for a bit. But I'd been to their house in Norwich. It was no palace. There were boxes of books everywhere. They worked hard. And soon the rewards started coming for them. Books they'd published began winning prizes. They doubled their turnover by publishing less and better, and I hoped they'd stick with me.

If I wanted to do any promotion, I had to do it for myself. Self-promotion was completely against my nature, but I had to try to make the effort, just for the sake of the book. I'd worked hard on it, and wanted people to read it. I'd done the reading at the Castle, but nobody else had invited me to read.

I kept sending emails to a book shop in town and finally got a reply. They said they were trying to fit me in to their hectic schedule and would be in touch. Ian Rankin was coming, did I know? Paul Auster, too. I was looking forward to that one, even if he seemed to have gone off a bit in recent years. The events manager would be sure to keep me 'in the loop'.

A couple of weeks later I emailed her and she said that she was sorry that she'd forgotten about my reading. The good news for me, as she phrased it, was that the crime writer Val McDermid had fallen ill and so there was a slot free.

Readings weren't really for me. I'd enjoyed the night at the Castle but I didn't become a writer so I could do readings. I'd thought this might be the big one, a hometown gig. Yet hadn't I been here before, when I'd done a reading with David Gaffney at Central Library and the little sod had stolen the show?

I wrote so much that I always found it hard to decide what to read. It had been the same at the Castle. I wasn't one of these performance poets who read the same five poems from memory for twenty years. I was always about the next piece of writing, that was what excited me. I wrote something every day, be that a poem or a short story or a bit of a novel, and that was all I thought about. I wasn't savvy. I just wrote one thing after another, developing all the time. I thought of myself as an artist. I watched programmes about artists more than writers. There was one with this bloke from Leeds, Norman Ackroyd, and it showed his day, how he got up early in the morning, wandered downstairs to work, then swanned off to the pub before coming back and working all evening. That was all I wanted from being a writer, that freedom, it was all about being free, and yet because I made no money I had to work in all these shit jobs, and I was no good in any of them because a writer was all I wanted to be, all I could be.

I finally decided what I was going to read, and practised in the living room. I read it aloud to Hermann. It was good writing, but already I was bored with it. How did writers do that, read old stuff over and over? That always felt like death to me. By the time something you've written gets published it is fucking ancient to you, if you've worked hard enough on it, and you are utterly sick of it.

When I got to the bookshop I asked the lad on the counter where I went for the reading.

'Oh, it won't be starting for a while yet.'

'Okay. But where do I go?'

'Like I said, doesn't start for a while yet. I don't think the author is here.'

'I'm the author.'

'You are? Oh right. Just go upstairs then.'

'Thanks.'

I went upstairs and found what appeared to be the room for the events. There was nobody in there. No microphone, no chairs out, no trays with wine glasses on. I shuffled around in there then went back to the counter.

'Who do I speak to about the reading?' I said, to a girl who looked about twelve and was making a big deal about putting books on a shelf.

'The manager?'

'Are you asking me or telling me?'

'The manager?'

'Okay . . . and how do I get in touch with the manager?'

She sighed and put the books down on a trolley. Then she walked over to the counter and picked up the phone and dialled it. As she did so I looked for my new book in the fiction section. It wasn't there. Or on the trolley.

'I've been told that the manager has gone home,' she said.

'Okay well who do I speak to about the reading?'

'The reading?'

'Please stop doing that upward inflection.'

'I'm sorry?'

'Look . . . I'm supposed to be doing a reading in about twenty minutes.'

'I don't know about it, sorry.'

I gave up on her and went back into the events room. All the chairs were stacked at the back and I started putting them out. Twenty would be enough, I was realistic. And I guessed I could manage without a microphone. I put a chair and table at the front, and then placed my copy of the new book onto the desk.

With about five minutes to go one of the booksellers ambled in.

'Oh, you sorted the chairs then?'

'Yes.'

'Did you put them all out yourself?'

'Yes.'

'Good effort.'

'Thanks.'

'What's your book?'

I showed him.

'Oh right. What's it about?'

I'd always found this a tricky question. 'The human condition,' I said.

'But is it like crime or . . .'

'Literary fiction.'

'Literary fiction?'

'Yes.'

'Okay, well, good luck with that.'

'Will there be any wine?'

'Wine?'

'Yes, wine.'

'No, that's for the proper writers. I mean, the well-known ones, you know. You're replacing Val McDermid, aren't you?'

'Well, she's not well, I believe.'

'There would have been wine for Val McDermid.'

'Good to know.'

'Okay, well, anything else you need just let me know.'

'Thanks.'

'You need to be out by eight.'

'No problem.'

When he left, I sat there looking at the empty chairs. Then I realised there were no posters or signs up or anything, so got up and propped open the door and stood there waiting. I got a text from Scoie that said he and Shackie were downstairs, so I gave them directions.

As well as Scoie and Shackie, there was my old mate Jammo and his Mrs, another bloke called Rennie that I used to work in a warehouse with, and then my poetry mates from Fuel, Ron and Bill. An old pal from school, Slogger Delaney, also turned up. He'd put on a wee bit of weight over the years but looked pretty much the same. He'd just got married and turned up with his Mrs, who seemed excited to be there. I'd told him about the book on Facebook and was glad of his interest. I knew all nine people in attendance.

After the reading, Ron and Bill headed off. It was unusual for either of them to venture out of the suburbs, and for Ron in particular it was a long slog back to Wythenshawe. So, it was me, Scoie, Shackie and Rennie that went to Corbieres for a drink. Maybe we could still make a good night of it. I'd asked Slogger and his Mrs but they both had to be up early for work the next morning, and the same was true for Jammo and his wife. They both bought a book off me though, and I was grateful for that. It meant I could get a round in.

Corbieres had long been known to have the best jukebox in Manchester, but I looked through it and it wasn't that great a choice, and half the time the music that played was skipping anyway. Nevertheless, we sat in a corner and drank our pints. The reading had been anti-climactic, to say the least, and apparently nobody had been able to hear me without a microphone. Now that the jukebox wasn't working properly it all felt a bag of shit, and there was no point trying to deny it. Scoie and Shackie bought copies of the book before heading off, which made me feel a bit better, and that left me and Rennie to catch up about the old warehouse days.

'So then, this is the literary high life, is it?' said Rennie.

'Yep,' I said.

'How are sales going?'

'Er . . . it is hard to say.' I hated that question. How could I know the answer? I'd never even had a royalty cheque. Did people think I got a text message or something, every time a book was sold?

'Long way from the warehouse,' he said.

'Sure is.'

'You know they knocked it down?'

'I saw that, yeah.'

'Moved us down Fairfield Street, nearer the Manky Way.'

'I know.'

'You did well getting out.'

'Thanks.'

'Always knew there was a bit more to you.'

'You ever see any of the people we worked with?'

'Well, you know Alan died, don't you?'

'No, I didn't.'

'Cancer of the balls.'

I didn't know what to say. When he was my foreman, I'd hated the cunt, but you wouldn't wish that on anyone.

'Anyone else?'

'Baz has retired, still lives on Edge Lane in Droylsden. Think Chris is running his own business somewhere. Got a hardware shop in Reddish. Er . . . Billy? Was Billy there when you were there?'

'One of the drivers?'

'Yes, that's right. He's running a boozer in Bury. You remember that bird Claire that was on reception, dumped you?'

'She didn't dump me. And anyway, she got together with that Daniel, didn't she?'

'That's right. Well, they are still together. About four kids.'

'She was fit.'

'Massive tits.'

'Was that Claire or Chloe?'

'Claire, if it's the same one we're on about. She's piled on the pounds.'

'You remember Bourney, the big boss?'

'Used to go with the hookers?'

'That's right. Well, we all did, didn't we?' he said, smiling. 'They found him in his car on Buxton Street. Heart attack. Rumour is, he had his pants round his ankles.'

'Well he was always at it.'

'You remember Big Plums? Got laid in the end. We all went out on the piss to celebrate. Married her as well.'

'Pleased for him.'

'Yeah he's calmed down a lot.'

'He needed to.'

'Did we ever have a leaving do for you?'

'No.'

'Didn't we go to the Bull's Head?'

'Not that I remember.'

'I think we did. Was a good night, wasn't it?'

I hadn't gone in on my last day, but I couldn't be arsed correcting him and just drained my pint. He went to the bar and came back with four pints, two each. He was always generous in that way, and he was the one guy from the warehouse I'd kept in touch with.

From Corbieres we walked up to Night and Day and Rennie started on the rum and black. Soon there was purple all around his mouth. It was just like the old days. I stayed in there with him until I'd spent the money from the book sales, and then we just seemed to run out of things to say. I gave him a hug when I left but I could have been anyone to him at that point, he was so pissed.

I walked down Oldham Street and across the concrete cock-up of Piccadilly Gardens. I sat on the 41 and listened to some Oasis on the phone, but I wasn't in the mood for it. I put some Tom Waits on instead, listened to a song written from the point of a view of a hooker. It was a great little song, like a short story.

As the bus passed slowly through the Curry Mile in Rusholme, I thought of how I used to go there with the warehouse lads at Christmas. How some of them just used to try and kick off, get in fights as a way of celebrating the festive season. I thought of how well I'd done to get out of that warehouse. I wondered how it would have turned out had I stayed there. This cheered me up a bit and then I thought back to the reading. Why were they always so fucking anti-climactic? I guess it was because nobody thought as much of my writing as I did. There had been more of a response from Hermann. I said to myself that I'd stop expecting anything from readings.

I was feeling sorry for myself as the bus passed the Christie hospital. It felt like Manchester had done nothing for my writing. People were still more interested in writers who had been dead for years, like Anthony Burgess, who hardly ever lived in Manchester anyway. They had a centre for him, and what started out as a way to keep his name alive turned into a corporate money-making exercise, using a dead writer's name to make dosh. They made beer called Clockwork Orange and Earthly Powers. What a crock of shit that was. I'd read three or four of his books and found the non-fiction to be the best. But none of his writing came from the heart, it was all from the head, an intellectual display.

My writing was supported by publishers in Cromer, Norwich, Northumberland, Wales, Plymouth, Salford. Never in Manchester, where the two biggest publishers were run by men from Oxford and Cambridge. I was Mancunian by accident of birth and beyond being a City fan didn't give a shit about it.

I waited for the book to get reviewed. There were no reviews. Nobody read the book, it sank like stone, and there were no royalty cheques. What made it more difficult was that I knew it was good. If only people had read it.

Sometimes people asked me if I had an agent. My response

was that ten per cent of fuck all is fuck all. But the real answer lay in the fact that almost all literary agents work within a few square miles of each other in London. I'd once sent a novel to one of the big agencies and the feedback showed that they just missed the whole point of the story. In broad terms, it was middle-class feedback on a working-class novel. And anyway, why should I have to travel to London to meet someone about my book? I wouldn't have anything in common with any of those people. I fucking hated London. We'd gone there once for a City youth team match. I was on a bus and wanted to ask the driver something. I went up to him, spoke through the glass at him and he told me to stand back, said that I was in his 'crash zone'. I just wanted to ask him directions. London seemed the coldest place in the world, the people desperate, rushing around, heads down.

Hermann had been hibernating, and I expected him to wake up any time soon. I didn't keep track of dates or anything, but I guessed he must be due to make an appearance. I waited. Eventually I looked in on him. I pulled back the hay and lifted him out slowly, but there was no movement, nothing. He never had done much except stroll around the garden tied to a long piece of string, eating as much plant life as he could stomach and shitting everywhere. Now he wouldn't be doing that any more. I thought of how much he enjoyed being stroked on the head, and the contentment he seemed to have in the slow lane. I read on Google that sometimes a tortoise can seem dead when it is just hibernating, but I gave him a couple of months beyond when he should have re-emerged, and he didn't. I couldn't bring myself to get rid of him at first. I thought of the day I brought him home, how he scrabbled from one end of the cardboard box to the other, at surprising speed, trying to get out. Just dumping him in the wheelie bin seemed harsh. And I couldn't decide which colour bin he belonged in anyway. I took him down to the river near the motorway bridge at Northenden. I walked down the bank, just downriver from the weir, placed him into the water, and watched the shell sink like a stone.

The next day I walked in to my shift at the mail centre, down Oldham Road, past the Chinese supermarket and the car wash. I dropped my stuff off in the room with the broken tumble dryer, put my high-vis on and my gloves, went for a quick piss and then walked onto the shop floor. And there she was, Zlata, on the conveyor, throwing mail into sacks, every bloke that walked past staring at her. At break time, I went over to one of the brightly lit seating areas that passed for a canteen. She was glugging from a big bottle of water. It was like she'd never been away.

'Good to have you back,' I said, smiling.

'Is it?'

'How is the baby?'

'Luka? He is fine.'

'He at home?'

'Yes, of course.'

'You have a baby-sitter?'

'Yes. My mum is here.'

'Oh right. Do you think we could go for a drink later?'

'I will think about it.'

'Okay great. My tortoise died.'

'What? Are you insane? We'll talk later.'

I waited outside. The cars passed by along Oldham Road. The lights from the chippy stretched out and illuminated a bus stop where a wino lay in a sleeping bag. In the distance, there were high-rise flats, just a handful of lights on. As usual, Zlata was brushing off the new guys.

'Nothing changes,' I said.

'No, it doesn't,' she replied, unsmiling.

'It must be difficult having to deal with that all the time.'

'Not now.'

'Why?'

'Why? Why? I tell you why. It is because I have a baby.'

'Oh right.'

'But it can work in my favour. If I want them to go away.'

In Gulliver's, we sat opposite each other, the table between us just as it had been on the night when we'd first had a drink. She had a pint, the same as me. She drank it pretty quickly, and when she went to the toilet I could see she was a bit wobbly.

'So, is your mum staying here?'

'For a while, yes. But then we go back to Bosnia.'

'I see.'

'I am saving money first.'

'So how long will you be here?'

'Few months. Maybe I will find man with a good job. Security for me and Luka. Not like here.'

'That's a shame.'

'Shame? Yes, it is. Get me another drink.'

'Okay.'

'You could come to see me in Bosnia,' she said, when I came back.

'Yeah, maybe.'

'You won't come. I know you. I know men like you.'

'How much is a flight?'

'You won't come. What is the point? You are stupid.'

'Calm down.'

'You tell me to calm down? I am an educated woman, master's degree in politics, journalist in Bosnia. What are you? Mail man? Ha ha!'

'I'm a writer.'

'You are not a writer.'

'I am.'

'You are not. Bulgakov is writer. Kundera. Borges. These are writers.'

'They are good writers, I agree.'

'The poems you sent me. I tried to be kind. But they are awful. About my ass? You call that poetry? You are a boy. You always objectify women. You are not a writer. A writer does not write about a woman's tits, boobs, whatever you call them. He writes about the soul. You are not a writer. You mail man. Ha ha!'

'Why are you being like this? I told you I don't write like that any more.'

'Oh, the writer is sensitive? Ha ha!'

'I'm a nice guy.'

'You are not nice guy. Get me another drink.'

'Why should I?'

'Okay I go. You sit down, save your money, little boy.'

I felt like going home, but I waited. There was a beer in it.

'You are not a nice guy,' she said, putting my pint on the table.

'I try my best.'

'You are typical man. You say you love me so we have sex. And after we had sex you would leave. I wouldn't see you again.'

'I never said that.'

'Ha ha! Every man is the same. You know the first man for me? My virginity? He raped me. Then I lived with a man. Rochdale Road. He beat me. Dragged me down the street by my legs. Threw me out into the street. I had to live in a hostel.'

'You told me. I'm sorry about that.'

'You are not sorry. My dad used to beat me. He used to beat my mum. As a child I saw it. Men are pieces of shit. I think I am going to be a lesbian.'

'Seems a bit radical.'

'Men are pieces of shit. They want sex. That is all. They don't know love. Luka will have all love in the world from mum and me. He will be different. I will meet another woman. I like women. Look at the barmaid. I have seen you looking. I love big breasts too, you see.'

'Don't tell me that.'

'You like lesbian? You think of me with her, yes?'

'Don't be daft.'

'You think of me on top of her. Do you think my breasts are as big?' she said, arching her back.

'Hard to tell.'

'Ha! You are a boy. A little boy. And you are not a writer. Never will be. So, don't email your silly poems about my ass any more, okay? I don't need a little boy. I have little boy already. I need a man. No, I don't need a man. I need a woman. Women are great.'

She got up and headed for the toilet. I finished my pint and left.

That weekend I walked past my old primary school. The original red-brick building was still there, though the windows were double glazed now. There were still the two entranceways, one with 'Girls' written above it, the other with 'Boys'. It all seemed so tiny. There were a couple of portacabins added. The old Dombovand's sweet shop was just another house, the big shop window bricked up. Red Hall Church was still there, though the building was completely new, and when I crossed over Audenshaw Road and walked up the stone steps the reservoir still looked impressive.

I'd jogged around that reservoir in the mornings, getting fit for the football, the frost nipping at my legs as I overtook dog walkers at a sprint. Did you ever do that, just break out from a jog into a sprint, see how fast your legs can move you?

Sometimes on those mornings I would come trotting down the steps that led down from the reservoir, see a girl getting into her car. She used to put the seat belt between her tits and it really turned me on. I always wanted to talk to her. I saw her on a night out in Ashton-under-Lyne, in a nightclub called The Love Shack, where they always played a song called 'Love Shack'. She was standing there with her friend. Her handbag strap bisected her tits. I stood there with Shackie and Scoie, necking one beer after another, getting up the courage. When I stumbled over I slurred my words, and though she'd tried to listen, she soon left with her mate.

The Pitt and Nelson, Yuppies, Love Shack, Molly Malone's, Yates's, the Loose Moose. I'd go to these places in Ashton with Scoie and Shackie, after a few pints in the Birch, and sometimes Pete Booth came along too. In the Birch there were a few gold leaf tables either side of the pool table. The door let in a draft because it was kept wedged open for passing trade. Indian taxi drivers played the fruit machines.

On the jukebox it was four songs for a quid, and I got up

and wandered over. I pressed the arrow buttons one way and then the other, reading the track listings on the inlay sleeves of the albums. I looked carefully at the letters and numbers and then put the combinations in. The CDs shifted around inside the glass box as I made my way back to the table, and we listened to the tunes. They weren't any of mine. It was then I noticed an older man in the tap room, smiling across at me and pointing at the other jukebox.

In Ashton, we'd watch as people snogged each other, and we got pissed and very occasionally one of us would get off with a girl. Usually it was just a laugh, a drunken laugh, a breaking free from the shackles. It was supposed to be rough in Ashton in those days, but we never really saw any fighting or anything like that. At Christmas it was always rammed, the streets filled with pissheads and fit women.

I remember one night in Ashton, a few months after the football injury that cut short my career. It seemed a good idea to get arseholed. We trailed from bar to bar, jostling and struggling to get served, making our way through the crowds that flocked to Ashton in those days. After pissing in a side street, I stood before a shop shutter and pounded it with my fists, over and over, slamming that shutter with my hands clenched tight, punching properly so as not to hurt myself. I kept on punching, the shop shutter crashing and rippling, and Scoie and Shackie just stood there, looking around. A couple of policemen approached and Scoie went up to them.

'It's all right, he's just had too many.'

'He can't be doing that,' one of the coppers said.

'He's not punching anyone, is he?' I heard Shackie say. And then there was the sound of a scuffle around the corner and the coppers moved off.

We headed to the curry house. Poppadums, nan bread, chicken 'mad arse', the works. A jug of lassi. Scoie hated curry so had egg and chips. At the end of the curry they took my plate away and there was a ring of rice around it. Scoie and Shackie got up to leave. I followed them. Two of the lads working in the curry house rushed over to us, blocking the door.

'We forgot to pay,' said Shackie.

'We forgot. Yes, mate. Sorry, mate. How much?' said Scoie.

'Your bill is on the table, sir.'

'Okay sorry, chief, we just forgot,' I said.

Ashton-under-Lyne. Another town that died while the city centre of Manchester was regenerated at the expense of everywhere else, a city centre designed to look magnificent on postcards. The tourists would never come to Ashton-under-Lyne. The trams were made to take you the other way.

The old flea market is still going strong, but most of everything else has gone. The indoor market destroyed by fire, repaired, but not the same. I remember the record shop on Old Street. Grumpy old guy working behind the counter, just his head above the stacks of vinyl. He had loads of great second hand albums, and I got my first Springsteen records in there.

Manchester was all about image, nothing about people. It was like when the Commonwealth Games came. I was excited to go, but couldn't get a ticket for what is now the Etihad. Eastlands, they called it then. I remember how they wrapped the old high rise flats in advertising so you couldn't see how poor it really was around places like Ancoats and Miles Platting. They've done it up a bit around there now. But go beyond that and there's nothing except discount stores and vape shops, people selling rags on markets stalls, crowds of the poor flocking to Smithfield market on Ashton Old Road on Sunday mornings for cheap fruit and veg.

They were trying to change Manchester with a load of glass buildings and horrible corporate shite, and bars and restaurants all over the place with no character at all. Parts of the city were given names that made me think I didn't know where I came from, whole wandering swathes of town where I walked in drunken bliss through the pubs and places I knew, only to get thrown off course by some new shimmering tower of glass. There were massive cranes rising to the skies, and roadworks everywhere, and places I'd walked so many times on auto pilot were fenced off, and I wondered where all the money was coming from. City centre Manchester didn't seem to fit with what I was seeing on the news, hearing on the radio. Everyone was skint, hundreds of people having to go to food banks including mates of mine, and people said they were scroungers for going to food banks when they were just feeding their hungry kids. People said things like, 'I would never go to a food bank,' and there was no empathy anywhere, the Tories kept trotting out their lies, and with all these people struggling, and myself working in the mail centre, Manchester kept growing and growing, one shiny glass tower after another blocking the sky, joining the dreaded Beetham Tower on the skyline. The Beetham Tower, not so much a monument to progress as a phallic monstrosity that said 'Fuck you' to everything in its shadow. When it is windy that tower sends a droning howl across places like Hulme and Salford, a noise and a high rise right out of JG Ballard. When it was being built, I sat on the balcony of the council block in which I lived, watching as it gradually took away my view of the sunset.

There were foodbanks in every city, benefit sanctions

everywhere. I went and watched the Ken Loach film, *I, Daniel Blake*. It hit the nail on the head. I hoped the silent Tory voters would go and watch it. Every time I put on the news there was something about the royal family: Charles opening a new building, the Queen waving from her big car, that monstrous palace behind her. I hated big houses, all that shit. I didn't see splendour in them, I saw the broken backs of the workers who'd built it.

I was tempted to go to a food bank myself, but I wasn't quite starving. I could live on the tenner a week I spent at Aldi. And I had plenty of time to write, all day in fact, until it was time for my evening shift at the mail centre.

Zlata came in one night wearing a T-shirt and no bra. You could see her nipples clear as day. When she walked past she frowned at me as I gazed. Time after time I saw her standing there, talking and laughing with some other guy. Then she chatted to the bloke from Bolton. I'd told her he was a twat and yet now here she was laughing and joking with him.

I tipped sacks onto the conveyor with increasing speed, even began to crack a sweat. And when I swopped to the conveyor I was flinging all the parcels into the baskets, keeping well ahead and having time to pause and rest. Hakan came over.

'Don't just stand there. Go over to the other side, help over there,' he said, pointing across to the other conveyor where Bal was hurling big boxes into the baskets over and over.

I went across to help her, and then I heard Hakan shouting.

'Whoa! Get back over here! Look at this!'

The conveyor on my side was now jammed full, the man doing the tipping standing there staring at me, and Hakan shaking his head. Zlata looked over and shook her head too, before turning around and chatting to the young lad working beside her.

'You can't get the staff!' shouted Hakan. 'You can't get the staff!'

'You told me to go over there!'

'Excuse me?'

'You told me to go over there.'

'Who do you think you are talking to?'

'I don't know. An idiot?'

'What do you mean with that?'

'Don't worry about it.'

'Don't worry about it? You will be worried when you don't get any phone calls.'

'What?'

'Carry on like this you won't be getting any shifts.'

I looked around. Both conveyors had stopped. Lots of people were looking over. Zlata was standing next to the bloke from Bolton. He nudged her with his elbow and they both started laughing.

'You really think I give a fuck, you dwarf?' I said.

'Oh. Mr Writer doesn't care, right? Thinks he's too good for here?'

'What?'

'Mr Writer. Cannot keep up. Gets upset. Artistic temperament.'

'Oh fuck off.'

'Sorry?'

'I said fuck off, you little Turkish twat!'

'Ha ha. Racist. That's it now, Mr Writer. Ha ha. You'll see.'

'See what?'

'You'll see. You'll see.'

'Well, you see that conveyor, you better get someone else on it.'

'No problem,' he said, waving Bal over. 'You see? No problem. Old woman. She can do it.'

I turned and walked away. I sat in one of the canteen areas and drank water from a plastic cup, waiting for Zlata. She had seen it all. I felt bad for Bal, maybe she was tougher than me, that's all. Of course, Zlata didn't come. I went into the changing room, took my coat out from under the dozens of others piled on top of it, and then waited for a permanent worker with a swipe card so I could get out through the sliding glass doors.

I walked down Oldham Street, past the adult shops, the cafés, the bars, Matt and Phreds jazz club, gorgeous old pubs like Gulliver's and the Castle. I looked in through the windows of Dry Bar and Night and Day, smiled to myself at the sight of youthful barmaids. I dropped into Night and Day, had a Jack Daniel's and ice while sitting at the bar. I had about £30 in the bank and set about spending it.

The next week I went in to the job centre and they told me I might be eligible for Universal Credit. I filled out the forms and didn't say anything about the mail centre. They also told me I could apply for council tax. The form for council tax was linked to a housing benefit application. I pointed this out at the job centre but they said I wasn't to worry, they wouldn't pay me twice.

When I noticed that they were paying me twice I tried phoning up to let them know. I couldn't get through the first time and didn't bother again. This meant that for a while I had plenty of money to live on and all the time in the world to write. I had to go into my local job centre once a fortnight to meet with my work coach. I fancied the arse off her and we both knew it, and she was really nice, never grilled me about my work search, just let me get on with it.

By now I'd had four collections of short stories published. I didn't know anyone who'd read as many short stories as me. But because I wasn't an academic I couldn't get a job teaching creative writing. One day I got a call from an agency in Stockport. They had seen my CV online and put me forward for a job working in Manchester libraries.

PART TWO

MANCHESTER LIBRARIES HAD been split into different areas, and I would be working in Manchester South. So, I could be either at Wythenshawe, Didsbury, Chorlton or Withington. It was £7.90 per hour, various hours, as and when required.

On my first day, at Wythenshawe, I sat at a desk to the side of the counter ripping the front pages out of books and looking out of the window at a succession of 43 buses heading for the airport.

'This isn't the dream,' I said, to Colin. He looked at everyone over an old pair of glasses, the right arm of which was taped.

'Excuse me?'

'Deleting books. This wasn't the dream.'

'No. I doubt it was. Welcome to Manchester libraries.'

'Not very busy, is it?'

'Never say that. Just you watch. They'll be flooding in later.'

'There won't be any books left soon,' I said.

'You're right. They got rid of loads at Central, without asking anyone. Did you know that? This job isn't what it was. At the end of the day they would be queueing up right down there,' he said, pointing across the library towards the lift.

'So, how do they decide what to get rid of?'

'We check how many times a book has been borrowed. If it hasn't gone out for however long they decide, then we delete it, take it off the system.'

'But how do you know that's right? People can just come in and look at it. Take it off the shelf, read a bit, then put it back.'

'That point has been made,' he said. He was reading the *Manchester Evening News*. The sports page, at the back. 'Anyway, my man Agüero is back on form.'

'Oh, you're a City fan?'

'Is there any other team in Manchester?'

'One in Trafford, I believe.'

'Oh, don't mention them scumbags.'

'I played for City.'

'I believe you, thousands wouldn't.'

'No, I did.'

'Very funny.'

'Long time ago.'

'Right, mate.'

Someone came to the counter and asked Colin for their library number. They had forgotten their library card and wanted to use a computer, and they needed the number to log on. He looked them up on the system and wrote their number on a slip of paper. Then he reminded them that the pin number was their date of birth.

'You seem to do that a lot,' I said.

'What's that?'

'Remind people of their library number.'

'Ours is not to reason why.'

'How hard is it not to lose a library card? Or just to make a note of the number?'

'I refer to my previous answer,' he said, flicking through the paper again. 'I hate that Mourinho.'

At break time, I had to look at my phone to remember the series of door codes that led to the staff room. The first thing I saw was a member of staff, Kerry, breastfeeding her baby. 'Don't mind me,' she said.

I sat down with a brew. The whole table was filled with food: toffee-flavoured crisps, a whole variety of brightly coloured bags filled with sugary treats, blueberry muffins. I looked briefly across at Kerry. She had stopped breastfeeding and was now just holding the baby, gazing down at it.

'Are these for the staff?' I asked, quietly.

'You new?' said Kerry.

'Yep.'

'Agency?'

'Yep.'

'Oh, don't worry. You don't have to whisper. Sean will sleep through anything.'

'Oh right. How old is he?'

'Seven weeks.'

'Wow.'

'Yeah.'

'I think he's the smallest baby I've ever seen.'

'Didn't feel that way coming out, let me tell you.'

'No. I can imagine.'

'Can you?'

'Well, no.'

'Zoe brings all that in,' she said, pointing to the snacks on the table. 'She's a feeder.'

'Might as well have a muffin then.'

'There's stuff in the fridge too. Melon and that. Trifles.'

'Splendid.'

'I'm on maternity. In case you're wondering what I'm doing here. Just done a bit of shopping. I'm shattered. Get a bit of peace here. You know my Gavin, takes the piss really. He says he's exhausted. Stressed. How can he be stressed? I'm the one who feeds the baby, picks up Kylie from school. Drives us everywhere. Makes all the meals. Reads to Kylie at night. And he's the one who's stressed?'

'Yep. I dodged a bullet there.'

'You not got kids?'

'No. That's what I mean.'

'Married?'

'No.'

'How come?'

'Er . . . it's a long story.'

'Someone out there for everyone. If Gavin can get married anyone can, believe me. Nah, I'm being tough on him really. He's a grafter.'

'Seems a decent job.'

'What, here? Yeah, it's all right.'

'People seem friendly.'

'Yeah. There's one or two you have to watch. Like . . . no, I won't tell you.'

'Oh come on, you can't say that.'

'You'll find out in your own time.'

'Fair enough.'

'The two managers here. That's all I'm saying. Do anything wrong, don't expect them to back you up. The public are always right, in their eyes. You been to any of the other libraries yet?'

'Only been here so far. Only started today.'

'Oh right, didn't realise. You must be replacing Georgina then?'

'No idea.'

'Right snotty cow she was.'

'How come she left?'

'Some sort of redundancy thing. Not a full redundancy,

I don't think. But her husband is loaded so she can retire.'

'Everyone seems fine, like I say.'

'Just watch the managers.'

'I just take people as I find them.'

'Yeah, probably the best way. Anyway, I've got to go to the post office yet. Then Asda. Then I go for Kylie. And then I have to sort the tea out. I tell you, when I come back here it will be for a rest. I'm not joking either.'

'Well I better go back. We get twenty minutes, right?'

'Yeah. Was half an hour until someone at Chorlton stuck their oar in.'

'Oh right.'

'We had half an hour for years. Then someone came over from Chorlton, and because they only get twenty minutes over there, they put a complaint in. So now everyone only gets twenty minutes.'

'I see.'

'And he's the manager at Central now. Work that one out.'

'What's he called?'

'Nigel.'

'Right.'

'Watch your back with him.'

'Okay.'

'He'll be all nice and smiley to your face, but he's a two faced so-and-so.'

'Thanks for the tip. Better go.'

'Yeah, you can still get half an hour sometimes, depends who's in.'

'Okay, cheers. See you later.'

'See you later.'

The library was part of the Forum Centre. There was

a gym, with a swimming pool. There was also a college, a chemist and a newsagent. I stood outside on my afternoon break. The sky was filled with a steady drizzle. Aeroplanes went up through the clouds. Buses splashed slowly through the station. My phone rang. Some twat on about PPI. The bloke next to me was having a fag.

'PPI?' he said.

'Yeah.'

'I just tell them to fuck off.'

'Well they're just doing their job, I guess.'

'You work in the library?'

'Yeah. Just on a break.'

'You used to be able to go in a library for a bit of peace and quiet.'

'Oh, I know,' I said.

'Now it's full of screaming kids. This mum came up to me and said if she could use the chair next to me. I said yes. Another one came up for another chair. I said yes. Then another. And there's some daft woman in there putting on stupid voices and reading out kids' books and they are all screaming. And another woman comes in - she's late - and asks for another chair and I felt like screaming, take the chair! I think they thought I was working there or something. Anyway, I'm more stressed now than I was when I went in.'

'Yeah?'

'Anyway, I'm off.'

'Okay, chief.'

I went back inside. All the kids were still screaming. I looked at the rota. For the next half hour, I was down for tidying. I looked in the tidying book. The shelf number told me where the last person had tidied up to. When I got there, I couldn't see it as being tidy. I don't think people bothered.

I saw one of my books. *Pictures from Hopper.* It was the one where I used the paintings of the American artist Edward Hopper as inspiration. By the looks of it, it had been taken out once. But it was all self-service machines these days so it didn't always get a date stamp. Anyway, it was in there. In the wrong place. I put it in the right place between Italo Calvino and Angela Carter. Every time one of your books was taken out of the library you were paid ten pence, something like that.

I got to Waterstone's, in Birmingham, five minutes before the reading was due to start. It was a big event, plugged by the publisher and heavily shared by all four authors on social media. On Facebook, it appeared that many people were coming, but in truth there was hardly any fucker there. I doubted anyone in Birmingham had heard of me. Waterstone's sold ten or fifteen books, which wouldn't have been enough to cover the cost of paying any of the writers, even had we been getting paid.

I read alongside three other writers. We each took our turn. I was nervous. It was the worst I'd read in public for a bit, I found it harder when there were less people. I could barely be arsed.

'What is it like being with a smaller publisher, compared to one of the big boys?' came one of the questions after.

'It works well for me,' I answered. 'They do a good job with the book, it looks great, and I don't have an agent, so there's no pressure, no deadlines, and my publisher pretty much publishes what I send them, there's no faffing about. Although saying that, I had an editor last time. He lives around the corner so that works well for me. I still haven't figured out how to make money though.'

'Well that ties in with my next question. What would you do if you were approached by a bigger publisher?'

'I turned them down,' said one of the other writers. 'After my Costa shortlisting I was approached by a number of the big publishers, and, like I say, turned them down.'

'Why?' I asked her.

'I like who I'm with. Better the devil you know, sometimes. And they've been good to me.'

The questions droned on. Some people could have sat there all night. I wanted to go to the pub. Finally, we did, some corporate dive near the train station. After necking a pint, virtually in one, I asked one of the other writers about her new novel.

'Yeah, it's getting there. But I've kind of got side-tracked into poetry at the moment. Frost.'

'I dip into poetry. Used to be Bukowski. Now I like James Wright, I think he's my favourite. Writes about the Ohio river and stuff like that. And Jim Harrison's prose poems. Oh, and Philip Levine's ones about working in car factories in Detroit. Love Levine.'

'Oh right. I don't know them.'

'*What Work Is*, by Levine, that's great. Then there's always Bukowski. He's good. He hates people and that, but don't throw the baby out with the bath water. He talks sense about being alive. Apart from that I just read poems here and there. I like poems rather than poets. Les Murray said that.'

'I like that idea. You seem to like poetry more than prose.'

'Well, it's all about art, isn't it? Being an artist. That's the thing. Bukowski's good, I mean the best books like *The Days Run Away Like Wild Horses Over the Hills.*'

'Yeah, I think I've heard of that one. But isn't he sexist?'

'He hates all people. But yes. It's like *On the Road.* The way Kerouac talks about women isn't great. But the rest of that book is beautiful. Dig the Bukowski out if you have it. If you want to write from experience he's your man. It's kind of prose shaped like a poem. I think that's my favourite kind, although the poetry snobs call it chopped-up prose. At the end of the day I like a narrative. I mean, I don't know much about your life, if you've had a lot of experience or anything?'

'Yeah, you could say that.'

'Well that stuff is gold dust. Shows you haven't just been in the education system all your life. You like haiku poems? My mate Ron does a workshop on Friday afternoons. Can lapse into a beer session though, sometimes.'

'I'd like to read some more haiku.'

'Yeah, love haiku. Total opposite of Bukowski. Everyone goes on about Basho, but Buson is my man. Lovely paintings too. There's one of crows on a branch in the snow. Love Buson. *Today is a happy day, the mountain is covered in fog.* Something like that. Hang on, that might be Basho. Love that shit though.'

Everyone had to get home, and I was left alone in the pub. I stood at the bar, content in my own company, not feeling the need to look at my phone. I looked into my pint, sipped from it, contemplated. Sometimes I wished I'd been a smoker, just so I could have time to contemplate. But you couldn't smoke in pubs any more.

I crossed the road and got on my train. I sat by a window, listening to the Tom Waits album, *Small Change.* There was nothing to see through the window. I closed my eyes, listened to the whole album twice, thought about the anti-climactic nature of the reading. There are people outside the arts who think that if you get a book published or an album produced or have an exhibition of your paintings, that you make money, might even be famous. But the percentage of creative people for whom that is the case is tiny. Year after year I'd been slaving away at short stories and poems. I got by on the buzz of getting them accepted for magazines, and simply carried on in the hope that I would write something great one day.

It was the short story form I loved the most, and the public was never going to be interested in short stories, they didn't know how to read them or how they worked. They'd been fed on a diet of easy TV. But I liked to think that by writing them I was helping the form to stay alive. It wasn't a fucking talent show. I liked American writers like Raymond Carver and Richard Ford. The kind of guys you'd have a beer with. I read and read, continuing to find hope and ideas, even in the work of contemporary writers. I liked *Young Skins* by Colin Barrett. I met Barrett when he did a reading at Central Library alongside someone who had done a novel about boxing clubs in the East End of London. I never did get around to reading that. But I liked Barrett. Great writer, totally unpretentious. In a literary world where it seemed that talking a good game was all, he let his writing speak for itself.

I had noticed this thing about talking yourself up, explaining the way you wrote. I don't know if it is because there are more writers and musicians and artists around than ever before, but it seems you have to be able to talk the arse off your work, explain everything, and this will appear to lift you a little above the rest. This is the horse shit on top of which creative writing PhDs are piled. I knew someone who really struggled with a PhD. She said you could write your fiction, which was easy, but then you had to write 30,000 words on how you wrote that fiction. How can you extend, 'I made it up' to 30,000 words? It seems that that was what she was required to do.

Open Book, Bookclub, Front Row, I couldn't listen to any of those programmes without having my love of literature damaged. They never talked about the writers I loved or books I liked, and when they did talk it just sounded like bollocks to me. Everyone on Radio 4 talked in posh accents that alienated me from the start. People waffling on about books, academics adding a layer of bullshit to a perfectly accessible novel, and writers, positioning themselves cleverly in relation to their published output. Careerists, not artists. People just there to compete with others in terms of intelligence. Just read the book and shut the fuck up, that was my attitude. More to life than books anyway. I wanted to teach writing without being pretentious, but that seemed impossible at university level, and I waited in vain for the opportunity to share, creatively, what I'd learned over many years on my own.

Later in the week I went to the poetry night at Fuel. It was always a great night, and nobody ever made any money. I read some of my prose. People shuffled around as I did so. And then came the performance poets. There was a Scouser. He read poems about storytelling, about how pubs used to be before the smoking ban. Old ladies drinking halves of lager, old guys on rum and black. Characters called Jimmy Bling and Nana Bling, and he performed a devastating one about life in Tory Britain under Theresa May called 'Fuck All'. People had to come up the stairs to use the toilet in Fuel, and when the Scouser was on, they stopped at the top of the stairs to watch and listen before heading back down. Like all good performance poets, he read from memory helped by repeated performance. He waved his arms and engaged the audience with his lyrical rhymes of Scouse Land, a Scouse Land of the memory that no longer exists except in his books and performances.

A big bearded bloke read after, and he had the audience in stitches with tales of travelling across the U.S.A. getting pissed and reading his poems. There was one where he had a barrel of beer poured over his head in Omaha, Nebraska. Then there was a woman with black hair who read lustful and lust-filled poems of sensuous rhythm and evocative figurative language.

Ron was still there after everyone had left, packing away the remaining merchandise of hoodies and badges with pictures of people like Jack Kerouac, William Burroughs and Allen Ginsberg on, and slogans like 'War Is the Sound of Money Eating'.

We went and had a pint downstairs. It was quiet, just the regulars: a bloke in a baseball cap who sat at the end of the bar and went out for a smoke, another bloke who sat with his laptop and a bottle of white wine, a bloke with a beard who read the paper and waited for his brassy wife. It was the usual guys behind the bar too, the tall lad with the beard and beret and the lad with the floppy blonde hair who played in a band. We sat at a round table in the corner, just by the store cupboard, Ron with his back to the wall facing the front door. I sipped from my pint of Portland Ale, and looked out of the window at the world passing by down Wilmslow Road. Students went in and out of the Canadian Charcoal Pit.

The lights of the take-away were reflected in puddles on the pavement. Buses and black cabs rumbled past, the faces on the buses blurred by condensation.

'I used to come back from town in the dead dog van,' said Ron, before taking a glug from his bottle of Sol.

'What?'

'The dead dog van.'

'Never heard of that.'

'Well where do you think all the dead dogs are? There used to be a van. And we got in the back of it. Another time we got on the back of milk floats. It's a long way back to Woodhouse Park when you're walking. That was the days they had milk on the doorsteps. It would be freezing but you'd just nip in someone's garden and get a pint of milk and it did for your breakfast. Those were the days when blue tits used to peck the silver top lids off the milk bottles. But I don't remember feeling cold, though there was always frost on the ground. You ever had that? Coming home pissed in the early hours of the morning, the sun just coming up, the bright orange glow mixing with the silver of frost across the fields?'

'You should write some of this down.'

'Nah, don't do prose. Too easy. Novels are written by people who think they know everything, and know nothing. Poetry is where it's at. Like Corso said, all the rock 'n' rollers wanted the term 'poet'. 'Poeta' – they want it on their gravestones. Jim Morrison – poet. But yeah, those mornings, I miss them. I used to walk that walk, miles, all the way back through Withington and Didsbury and Northenden. Northenden Village as they call it. But it's part of Wythenshawe really. Always has been. Anyway, I'd walk by the Mersey for a bit, cut a corner in Northenden and go down past the Tatton Arms.

The sun shining on the weir, the water above it looking perfectly flat, the little green footbridge over the river reflected. When I was pissed everything looked like a Van Gogh. Still but swirling, you know? I'd stand by the river with my bottle of milk and then have a sit down on one of the benches around there, near that little park with the heron sculpture, and when I started to get cold I'd get up again and carry on walking, make my way through Sharston. Glory days.'

'Sounds like it.'

Sometimes at Fuel, Ron read poems about his mum and dad who'd died not that long ago, lovely little poems with specific details from his childhood. Other times he'd do his political stuff, left-wing socialist rants against the welfare cuts made by the Tories. Iain Duncan Smith and all those soulless bastards. People who signed the death warrant for thousands of disabled people who'd been on benefits. Those poor souls who killed themselves because it was easier than having to prove their disability over and over.

Out of the blue, I got a message on Facebook from Zlata. It had been sent at about three in the morning. It just said, 'I miss you.' I left it a day or two and then replied that I missed her too. She talked about the baby and we arranged to meet up. She said she was skint and invited me to her house. She'd moved to Northern Moor.

I got off the tram and walked into what looked like a council estate. Her house on Button Lane had a patch of long grass before it and over the road there was a row of shops with a take away called Sam's, an off licence, a Caribbean take away, a tanning salon and a launderette. The front windows of the house were blocked by thick blinds so you couldn't see inside, but when I sat in the living room, the light from the off licence shone across the road and through the frosted glass of the front door.

The Christian couple Zlata lived with, Dave and Linda, had been banging and crashing in the kitchen for the previous two hours and had made massive pans full of veg curry and rice. They offered me a plate, which I gratefully accepted. Then they filled a couple of tiny plates for themselves and ate them in silence at the tiny dining table in the corner of the living room.

'Are you in a church?' asked Dave.

'Me, no.'

'We welcome everyone.'

'Good.'

'Sunday evening. Every Sunday evening.'

'Right.'

'There's a podcast.'

'Oh yes.'

'You want to look?'

'No thanks.'

'I can find you the link.'

'Really doesn't matter.'

Why did the bible bashers always try to convert you? I had no problem at all with religious belief. I respected it – Catholics, Muslims, Buddhists, whatever. If it works for you do it. My god was the Man City striker Sergio Agüero. I worshipped at his feet on Saturday afternoons.

'You doing anything this weekend?' I asked Dave.

'Planning to go to Ordsall Hall.'

'Oh yes. What's that, like a country house?'

'Yes.'

'What is it, like black and white, what's that, Tudor?'

'Not sure. Worth a visit though.'

'You go for a pint after? Couple of nice boozers round there.'

'No, no, no. We don't drink. And we don't go to restaurants or cinemas and we don't go to pubs either.'

'Oh right. Why's that?'

'We just don't believe in those things, do we, Linda?'

'No.'

'And that is difficult for Linda. Her family love a drink, don't they, Linda?'

'Yes.'

'They are like that in Liverpool.'

'I've never been.'

'Don't, it's an awful place . . . I'm joking . . . well, kind of.'

I'd look at those people singing away on *Songs of Praise* and they seemed ridiculous to me, their mouths wide open like goldfish, rolling their heads in rapture. But I knew the score. They sang their hearts out and preached the bible but they were all shagging each other.

There was a bloke I had worked with in a bookshop a few years before. He was called Peter. Very knowledgeable guy. He knew about world politics and was always telling me about the imminent global recession. He was right, what he predicted was right, and he'd been saying it for ages.

The rumour was that if you went around to his flat and opened the door then books would fall out, he had so many of them in there. When I was working with him in the bookshop he had encouraged me to nick the books. He said our wages were so low that it was only right. They always wrote off a certain percentage of the profits to theft anyway. And those twats in the Oxford branch were getting paid miles more for doing the same job. Peter liked foreign writers: Orhan Pamuk, Michel Houellebecq, Gabriel García Márquez. But his favourite writer was Graham Greene and if you asked him what his all-time favourite novel was, he'd say *The Power and the Glory.*

I think Peter prayed every night. He had been brought up a Catholic and had almost gone full circle with it. He seemed to need it more as he got older. He wasn't married or anything, maybe that had something to do with it. He went to midnight mass at Christmas. Before I met him, I had thought religion was just a load of bollocks.

'So, what do you do?' asked Dave.

'I'm a writer.'

'Like what?'

'Short stories, novels, poems.'

'I hated poetry at school.'

'Me too.'

'So, what is your writing about?'

'Kind of autobiographical. Just change the names,' I said, smiling. 'Sometimes I forget to change the names.'

'But what is it about?'

'Varies.'

'But is it like crime, or . . .'

'Literary fiction.'

'Literary fiction?'

'Like Camus, Dickens. I can see them on your shelf.'

'Oh, they are Linda's, not mine. And I doubt she has read them.'

'I have,' she said.

'She doesn't waste her money on that stuff any more.'

'Well, yes, you've got the bible there, haven't you? Plenty

to be getting on with there. I must get around to reading it one day.'

I remember when they came to school with the Gideon's bibles. We were in pottery class with Mrs Neale. Me and Houghy used to throw the clay up to the ceiling and it stuck there, and then at random intervals during the class it would fall and we'd all laugh our bollocks off. We were a right couple of twats. But when the bible people came they talked in soft voices, and it all went quiet, and I found it very soothing.

'What's the notebook for?' I asked Dave.

'We copy out passages.'

'Oh right.'

Short stories, poems and novels were my bibles, I read them for wisdom and insight, and knowledge about how it is to be human. I thought the great books I read made me a better human being. Richard Ford's *The Sportswriter*, Steinbeck's *The Grapes of Wrath*, Kerouac's *On the Road*, Melville's *Moby-Dick*. Non-fiction: Steinbeck's *The Log from the Sea of Cortez* and *Travels With Charley*, and Peter Matthiessen's *The Snow Leopard*. Short story writers too: Carver, Ford, Cheever. And poets: Bukowski, Levine, James Wright. All Americans – fuck knows why, doesn't matter.

Zlata was finally ready. She'd put too much make up on, but it wasn't for me to say. It was her hair that took ages, she said. It was too frizzy, she said.

'What's the occasion?' said Dave, to Zlata.

'We are going for a drink in Didsbury.'

'Didsbury, very nice, I believe. But why do you have to dress like a prostitute?'

'Dave!' shouted Linda.

'I'm only joking,' he said. 'Where you headed?'

'Metropolitan, probably,' I said.

'Oh, you'll like it there, Zlata, lots of rich men.'

'Do you have some sort of filter, mate?' I said.

'What do you mean?'

'I know it's your house and that, but you don't have to be rude.'

'Zlata knows I'm only pulling her leg.'

'English humour,' Zlata said, to me, smiling.

'You ever been to Home, Dave?' I asked. 'Not the one in town, the one in Didsbury?'

'Yes.'

'I've read poetry there.'

'We don't like poetry.'

'No. I get that.'

'Nice church though.'

'Yes, it is.'

It made me laugh. You had these vicars and that, and loads of women too. And they had the cool ones on TV, young people, attractive women, and handsome men with long hair who looked a bit rock and roll even with the dog collar on. They were always wildly enthusiastic and incredibly irritating.

There was a mosque around the corner from where I lived. Packed out with cars on a Friday afternoon. People walking everywhere on the way out, walking in the road. It was like Maine Road, back in the day, coming out after the match.

I liked the congregation in the Kippax, the battle hymns, chanting, *Come on City, Come on City* over and over in a cramped corner under an old stand with a corrugated iron roof, with pillars blocking the view sometimes. The pungent smell of fag smoke and booze. Some bloke passing a hip flask. And when a goal went in there was a feeling of joy, especially if it was like a last-minute winner or something, and you'd be jumping around and hugging, sometimes even hugging some fat bloke you didn't know. And you'd see the fervour in the faces of all those men, all ages, plenty of them a bit drunk but so what? They were great people, those fans. I wanted to be one of the men that could bring something to those people, and now all I could bring was my writing.

I'd go to the Etihad sometimes with Scoie, when he had a spare season ticket. We'd always get there early, stand there, right at the back of the South Stand, way up in the sky. It was the cheapest season ticket in the stadium and the view was amazing. You could see the genius of Sergio from that height. The way he found space by just strolling around, and then burst onto the ball to score. Me and Scoie would stand there, praying for that. Praying in our hearts for a Sergio goal.

The next time I went to Zlata's, Dave and Linda were out. Her bedroom was above the kitchen. It was tiny. There was a little desk, a wardrobe, the bed and a coat stand. The washing machine was going in the kitchen below us. I asked her to open a window. I could hear blackbirds in the dusk. In the background, motorway traffic. On her bed, there were some cuddly toys. A duck, a pug and a ragged little cat.

'Where's Ryan then?' I asked her.

'Ha ha. He's gone.'

'Gone?'

'Well he's still at the mail centre but he's not interested.'

'That's awful.'

'I don't mind.'

'Does he help you out?'

'He gives me money sometimes,' she said, turning the

bedside lamp on. 'But we don't need him. He has many kids. Different mothers.'

'Yeah, you said.'

'Doesn't really care about any of them. So many men are just boys. No responsibility. But it doesn't matter. Maybe we go back to Sarajevo. My mum she wanted a grandchild for so long. She says she will pay.'

'Oh right.'

Luka began to cry and Zlata walked across to the cot. She picked him up and rocked him in her arms until he went quiet. Then she placed him gently back down.

Zlata turned to me and smiled. 'I don't want to talk about Ryan,' she said.

She put on a bedside lamp and closed the curtains. Then she lifted off her T-shirt. Stood there in bra and knickers. She looked incredible. We got in bed and she pressed up against me, and then she turned away, began crying.

'Last man before Ryan, he left me too. Hit me with a belt buckle, you see the scar?' she asked, turning her back to me. I could see it, a melted slash across the small of her back, visible even in the lamplight.

'I was in a hostel after that.'

'Sounds awful.'

'I want to live in a mansion.'

'Don't we all.'

'The woman used to live next door here, she lives in mansion now. Hale?'

'Hale. Yes, in Cheshire. How did she go from here to there?'

'Her son paid for it. I want to be rich.'

'What does he do?'

'He is a footballer.'

'What is he called?'

'Marcus Rashford.'

'Rashford? He plays for United. Hate to say it but he's good.'

'Proper footballer. Not like you.'

'Very funny. No, seriously, he played for Fletcher Moss Rangers, in Didsbury.'

'She has easy life now.'

'Just goes to show you.'

'She never has to work.'

'Shows anyone can make it. If you are good enough.'

'I bet she has a cleaner.'

She was lying on her back, the bra rising and falling with her breath. I kissed her belly and she turned away from me. The lamplight shone on the cuddly toys that I'd moved to the foot of the bed. I lay against her.

'No,' she said.

'Oh, come on,' I said.

'No means no.'

'Okay.'

I fell asleep. When I woke up I was shivering. I could still hear the motorway. Zlata woke and turned towards me, began touching me. I kissed her but she was sleepy. She started to touch me again but stopped suddenly. She pulled the covers off and turned onto her front. I looked at her arse and then got up onto my haunches and moved over. She pushed me away and I lay there listening to the cars.

When I left in the morning she gave me a long kiss, biting my lip quite hard. I walked across the grass outside her house, towards the row of shops, and then along Sale Road to the tram stop. I looked at the passing scenes, before changing trams at St Werburgh's Road. As the tram neared the football pitches at Hough End, I got off and went to watch one of the matches. Everyone seemed to be chasing the ball. There was a lot of shouting and swearing. The pitch was bobbly as fuck, patches of mud everywhere. The ball seemed heavy, the players slow. The ball got booted high up into the wind and swirled around. There was a penalty for an obvious handball. The player stepped up to take it and smacked it straight at the goalkeeper who shovelled it into his own net. There was a Cruyff turn that lifted my heart. Trams passed by behind the goal. The game finished. There was a scattering of applause.

I walked down Princess Parkway towards Southern Cemetery. I saw shops selling gravestones and balloons. I took a shortcut between the graves. They say Morrissey used to like this cemetery, or wandered around it anyway. There were graves in readiness all over the place, piles of soil next to them and the holes covered over with wooden boards.

The traffic on the parkway was busy. I crossed at the lights and headed back into Didsbury along Barlow Moor Road. Most days I'd see actors from *Coronation Street*, usually sitting outside a bar in the afternoon. I especially liked the trees and the birds in Didsbury, and the river and the parks. The people I was less sure about. They seemed cold, aloof, preoccupied with money.

I headed for the Art of Tea café. It was warm inside, and the waitress wore a black T-shirt and jeans. I sat at a table facing the counter. She came back and forth and I watched the way she walked. The tea was English Breakfast, loose leaf, came in a glass. Tea in a glass. What the fuck was that about? There were old songs playing by Fleetwood Mac. I asked the waitress how long she had been working there. She said about a year.

I liked the way that she stood there stretching, playing with her hair, leaning to one side, weight on one foot then the other, all the time watching me watching her in the mirror, on the wall behind the counter, next to the board with the specials written in chalk. The last time I went there, she came and sat next to me at the table facing the counter. She showed me a picture on her phone. A perfume she liked. *Angel* by Thierry Mugler.

At home, I looked at stuff on YouTube. I stumbled on a video of a very attractive young Scottish woman smiling right into the camera. It was a point-of-view shot. She seemed to be measuring me up for a suit, all the while talking in a relaxing, calming voice and gazing straight into my eyes. I felt tingles along my spine. I plugged some headphones in and the effect, the tingles, doubled in pleasure. She was called Heather.

I subscribed to her page, watched videos of her trying on jewellery, handing out books in a bookshop, washing hair, brushing her own hair. Sometimes she tapped things, rustled sheets of paper, all the time talking softly, descending now and then into a whisper. Sometimes she got close to the microphone and whispered into it and this chilled me out so much I got a bit addicted.

It was called Autonomous Sensory Meridian Response, or ASMR, and YouTube was full of people doing it. Usually attractive young women. I had experienced it on one or two blissful occasions throughout my life, without knowing that was what it was called, or that was what was happening. The first time I remember was at the dentist, of all places, on Guide Lane in Audenshaw, where a brown-haired woman bent over and examined my teeth, the folds of her white coat brushing against me, the calming voice well practised and soothing.

Another time I was having physio on my knee, and there was something about the way the physio talked. During the procedure, she was almost rubbing her breasts on me. She must have been struck off or something if she kept doing that. But why would you complain? I walked out of there feeling utterly blissful. Another time there was an Indian woman who worked in the local shop. Her voice was so relaxing and I loitered and listened as she talked to her customers.

Back in the library I was on a late shift with Colin. I stood at the counter, looking through the window at the 43 buses passing by.

'Love life is a nightmare,' I said to him.

'Oh dear.'

'There's this girl. Fancy the arse off her but she has a kid.'

'A familiar tale.'

'I think I should have made more of an effort. Too late now. Little lad, she's got.'

'It complicates matters.'

'Too late anyway.'

'Where does she live?'

'Northern Moor.'

'Oh aye?'

'Button Lane.'

'I know it. Just up from Moor Village. Used to go in a pub round there. The Yew Tree? Think it's a restaurant or something now.'

'Right.'

'Have you ever been married?'

'No. Dodged a bullet there.'

'Ha.'

'Are you?'

'No. Used to be.'

'Oh right. So, what went wrong, if you don't mind me asking?"

'No, I don't mind. Not at all, there's no secrets. She played away. I found out. And that was the end of that.'

'Ah.'

'Oh, I got my own back, but that was the beginning of the end of it, really.'

'Sorry about that.'

'These things happen.'

A borrower turned up, saying the self-service machine was broken. While Colin helped her out, I picked up a handful of books and shelved them. I put a James Patterson novel back on the shelf, next to nine others of his, then went back to the counter.

'Thing was, I married the wrong one,' said Colin. 'I always remember, on my wedding day, my old fella came up to me and whispered in my ear and said it wasn't too late for me to back out. But my mind was made up.'

'So, who should you have married?'

'A girl I knew for years. I remember my old fella told me she was the one. He told me I should have got together with her. He even kept saying that, even after I got married to the wrong one. And you know the funny story? I sent her a letter, saying I was getting married. And it came back to me, after the wedding. Return to sender. She never read it before the wedding. She never saw the letter.'

'What was in it?'

'What do you think? I told her how I felt about her. And she never saw it. And I got married.'

'You ever tried to find her?'

'Not recently. I did for a bit. After the divorce. But that's what I mean. Sometimes you don't know what you've got.'

'She might be on Facebook.'

'Oh, I don't do any of that social media shit.'

'Fair enough.'

'Wouldn't even know how. Tweeting and all that bollocks. Get a life.'

'Yeah. Things were easier before it, in a way.'

'What do you mean?'

'Well, ex-girlfriends putting pictures of themselves on there and that. There was a girl I used to go out with, Denise. She blocked me though. But you see the others on there, with their new boyfriends. Declaring undying love for each other. Announcing their relationships on Facebook. Pouting.'

'Sounds like a load of old rubbish.'

'Yes, it is. I'm only on there to plug my writing.'

'Oh yeah. Someone mentioned you're a writer. Poems and that?'

'Mainly short stories, but yes, some poems.'

'Hated poetry at school.'

'Yeah. But you don't have to rhyme these days.'

'Well that's a relief.'

'The other thing about Facebook is all these women on there, putting selfies of themselves.'

'Don't start me on selfies.'

'It's like, is that all there is to you?'

'My advice to you would be, though, for what it's worth, never go on a blind date.'

'Okay. Why not?'

'I mean, even if you've seen a picture of her and she doesn't look like the back end of a bus.'

'Yeah, meeting people online is dodgy.'

'This online stuff is all going to end in tears if you ask me. Nobody actually talks to each other any more. What is real isn't real, if you know what I mean.'

'I do know what you mean. But I've met a few women on Facebook. You can get to know them a bit first. Maybe that's what all the pouting is about. But I'd rather see something from their brains.'

'You make a valid point.'

'I find intelligence attractive.'

'It is. All joking aside.'

'Dead in here tonight.'

'What have I told you? *Never* say that.'

'Why?'

'They will be flooding in now. You wait.'

An old woman brought back a load of romance novels that I doubt she'd even read, and there was an Australian bloke and his wife going on about sci-fi novels and how they didn't have a TV. They gave me a long list of books I should read, and talked enthusiastically about sci-fi until about ten to eight.

After we locked up, and before Colin turned towards the car park, he looked at me over his glasses. 'Sorry you didn't make it at City,' he said.

'Cheers,' I said.

'See you tomorrow.'

'Yep. See you tomorrow.'

It was half eight before I got on the bus back. I got off on Palatine Road and walked the short distance home through Didsbury. I went past the synagogue, where the security guys at the gate always said hello when they were there, down past the entrance to the Albert Club and further down the road to my flat. I lived opposite a big house that had Egyptian statues in the garden. When people walked past at weekends they often stopped and stared before taking pictures. The statues weren't real. A bloke told me they were made of fibre glass, and had been used as part of an ice show by Torvill and Dean, filmed at the old Granada Studios on Quay Street.

The next night I went and saw a play at the King's Arms in Salford. I was trying to broaden my horizons but all they did was eat cold baked beans and it was freezing in there. On the way back to the tram stop I walked past what was now called 'Spinningfields'. Some twat in a daft suit dropped a load of coins in a homeless man's lap outside Costa Coffee and said, 'There you go.' Behind him, a woman in high heels was being held up by her tattooed boyfriend. His hair was glistening and parted, and his beard was like a bush.

The bright shining buildings that lined Spinningfields were symptomatic of what some people were calling regeneration. But all taste seemed to have gone from architecture. I was no expert. The buildings just looked shite. The city centre of Manchester has never been my Manchester anyway. The Haçienda, all the music mythology – when all that stuff was going on I was out on the piss in Ashton-under-Lyne or playing football on Platt Lane in Moss Side. But they kept building these tall glass monstrosities. A couple of ex-United players, multi-millionaires, had plans to demolish the old Sir Ralph Abercrombie pub and the Bootle Street police station to make way for two more of these shiny penis extensions that gave no thought to history, culture or surroundings. Just because you gave the building a name that has some historical significance to the city doesn't mean you give a toss about it, that stuff is just lip-service. I put my name down on a petition. I'd had a good night's kip in that police station, and the old pub was a beauty. I loved old pubs, such style to them, what with their imaginative names and painted, hanging signs, and inside, the gilt mirrors and glowing optics and marble walls, places where even the toilets were a work of art, bogs so good you might think twice before pissing in them. Boozers still hanging on like The Deansgate, The Briton's Protection, The Peveril of the Peak, The Town Hall Tavern, Sam's Chop House, The Lass O' Gowrie. Places with style, places where it was a pleasure to get shit-faced.

The hipsters tried to recreate the magic old pubs but they couldn't because it was all a front. Me and Scoie went in the old Abel Heywood pub in the Northern Quarter. We sat there for hours, drinking the Lowry ale, which was pretty good. Scoie had just told me about the night he got together with his wife, and there was a tear in his eye. Then a lad collecting glasses came. 'Pass me the glasses,' he said. Not a 'please' or a 'thank you' in sight. You go in any rough-arse pub and the bar staff have manners. But in these middle-class gaffs the sense of entitlement pervades all.

We drank for a bit longer, and then the lad came and put a laminated sign on our table that said, 'Reserved for 4.45'. Scoie wanted to argue the toss but we moved towards another table. It had another sign on. We stood there grumbling. The manager frowned at us from a table in the corner. We finished our beers and left. This was the Northern Quarter. Generic money-making boozers dressed up as heritage by hipster shysters who sit in the pub totting up the cash on a laptop.

Didsbury library was a ten-minute walk from my flat. I went down Parkfield Road South and Oriel Road and I was there. I walked round the back and rang the bell and Lorraine, the manager, let me in. I went upstairs to the staff room and dropped off my coat and came back down the stairs and stood behind the counter next to Jhumpa, Dakshi and Stephen. Stephen had just come back with the newspapers and was talking with an old Asian guy about the test match going on between England and Pakistan. Jhumpa and Dakshi were talking too, and I stood there watching the door, waiting for the punters to come in.

Stephen was a musician. He'd had some success about ten years previously, touring with more famous musicians and making a name for himself in the crowded singer-songwriter market. Now he was working three days per week in the library and spending the rest of his time doing gigs with various bands as well as continuing his sensitive songwriter stuff. I had a listen to some of it on SoundCloud. It was good. Reminded me a bit of Ray Davies, all quirky lyrics about the suburbs. They loved him in Chorlton, with his horn-rimmed specs and hipster beard. On his lunch breaks in the library, he'd go out onto the roof with his guitar and sing songs to the birds. He loved his food too, was always knocking something up within the limited confines of the staffroom kitchen.

The library was surrounded by delis and cheese hamlets and butcher's shops and fishmongers but I really couldn't be arsed with all that. The country seemed obsessed with food, the great British waste of time. Cooking, that antidote to having a pulse. Is there anything more boring? Most people just want to be like everybody else.

There was one show. Nigel somebody or other. Old bloke in glasses. Stood in this vast spotless kitchen and rambled on about herbs. He said he liked to be spontaneous and buy whatever he wanted every time he went shopping. I hated him. He went into a deli and talked to the man behind the counter. They went into his pantry. It was huge, overflowing with pots and jars of food. They started going on about avocados.

After that there was Nigella Lawson's ludicrous food porn. Soft focus nonsense played out to a soundtrack of comatose jazz for middle-aged masturbators. I wondered what planet these clowns were on. The only one I liked was Rick Stein. With him it was like the food was just a part of your life, not your whole life. The others seemed desperate, as though the relentless focus on food was what kept them from shoving their heads in a deep-fat fryer.

I liked something that took more time to eat than it took to make. So, I kept going to Aldi and coming back with the most basic food I could find. One day I showed Stephen a box of cup-a-soups and I thought he was going to vomit. He faffed about for half an hour of his lunch break, ending up with something tiny on his plate that he ate within minutes. When he finished it, he just looked sad.

I went to see one of his bands in the Railway. This was his rap band, and they sang a really funny song about cats and dogs on a council estate. They had a guitarist who sounded a bit like Tom Morello, the guy who played with Springsteen. It was the usual thing after a gig, you told them how good they were. But it was like everything else, there were so many bands, so many writers, so many artists, which ones to choose?

Jhumpa was from Bangladesh, and Dakshi southern Pakistan, I forget exactly where. They had been moved into the library jobs by the council after being made redundant at the nurseries where they'd worked.

I was working alongside Dakshi when a man gave her details of his reservation.

'And what's your name?' asked Dakshi.

'Fitzhugh.'

'Can you spell that for me, please?'

The man sighed heavily and then spelt the name out quickly.

'I'm sorry but can you repeat?'

Again, the man sighed heavily.

'Slowly, please.'

The man was becoming red-faced. 'I haven't got time, look I've come in for my reservation. It should be on the shelf. Can you do it, mate?' he said, looking over at me. 'Fitzhugh?'

I looked at Dakshi and she was fine with it, and so the man came over to me while Dakshi stamped some books for another borrower. The self-service machine was on the blink again.

'Fitzhugh. And the first name?'

'James.'

'Okay, yes, here you are.'

'Thanks. It is always easier when you speak the same language, isn't it?'

'I guess so.'

'I avoid her,' he said, lowering his voice.

'She does her best.'

'She ticks a box, doesn't she?'

'I don't think that has anything to do with it.'

'Oh, come on. We all know how it works. If it was up to me I'd put a wall around Didsbury.'

'Your book isn't in yet, I'm afraid. Did you say you'd had an email to say it had arrived?'

'No, no. But I ordered it two weeks ago. How long does it take usually?'

'It varies.'

'Okay. Okay. Thanks a lot. I know who to come to next time anyway.'

I looked over towards Dakshi, who was smiling politely as another borrower spelled out their name. It was hard enough if English was your first language, the way people just spat out the letters.

'It's a pain the way they expect you to be able to get their names down,' I said.

'Oh yes. It's difficult.'

'Bunch of arseholes,' I whispered.

She smiled.

'All of them,' I said, as a borrower approached. 'Ah, sir, good morning to you,' I said, in a sarcastic tone. I looked over at Dakshi, who had begun giggling.

Jhumpa, on the other hand, was rude back to them, and people were always complaining about her. She told me, as did Dakshi, that she'd much rather still be working in the nursery. But that she didn't really have a choice. And then I found out that Jhumpa was a writer, had had poems published in a Dhaka newspaper and was quite famous in Bangladesh.

By now my shifts at the library were all over the place. Sometimes I was at Wythenshawe, sometimes at Didsbury, sometimes at Chorlton, rarely at Withington. It was a stupid idea to move staff round like that, just made the job more difficult. It was a shit job, really, but I liked the people I worked with. One time at Chorlton, I went out for lunch with Simon, who'd been working there for years and had actually qualified as a librarian in the days when that meant something. He got the beers in, and started going on about the library.

'Some of them don't even know where they live. You ask them their date of birth and they don't know that either. You ask them their kids' names and they can't remember. Seriously, I'm not joking. You think I'm joking? Just wait, it will happen to you. The world has gone mad. At least in here we get no mither. Yesterday was mad. Angela said she had a nightmare last night. Bloke came in and he ordered five inter-library loans. At ten to five. Expert at Greek mythology but can't grasp that we need to go home. Do they think we just want to stay here all night? We don't get paid enough for this. At least we can come in here. But don't broadcast it. It's our own time anyway, there's fuck all they can do. I'm having another one. What's that you're having?

'Pomodoro sauce.'

'Thought you asked for fish and chips? Pomodoro sauce, what the fuck is that all about? You want a bag of crisps with it, fill you up?'

'Yep.'

'Fuck off.'

He came back with the beer and took up where he'd left off. He spoke in monologues, rarely made eye contact.

'I'm in the union and so as part of that we get a vote. Unison. I'm going for Corbyn. I know what people say but if I vote for him I can live with myself. He's been treated like shit. You don't even see him in the media. It's atrocious. He's not even that left wing. I mean, he's not Stalin. But you don't even see him. He sat on the floor on a train because there weren't any seats and they had a go at him for that. They take the piss out of his suits. His beard. And then you get that cunt Farage. Dropped us in the shit, and yet he's still taking a wage from the European Union. It's like he's standing there waving his dick at us. You know what I mean?'

'Yes, I do.'

'Can't live on these wages. Well maybe I could if I didn't have a pint every night but I'd go mad if I didn't have a pint. How much have they started you on?'

'About eight quid an hour.'

'That probably works out to about thirty pound a week less than me. And I've done seventeen years, nearly eighteen. None of my pay rises have matched inflation. In some ways, I'm on less. It's okay this job for maybe two or three years but in the end, it just grinds you down dealing with these muppets all the time. I wonder, can they even eat or does someone feed them all with a fork when they get home? For some people, it's like they're addicted to crack. And we're here to serve them. I mean, it's crazy. They're addicted to this place. Anyway, I'm having another.'

When he came back I still had most of my first pint left.

'Old fella I used to live with. Had a tracheotomy but it was too late. He was a good friend of mine. He was a real chain smoker. He gave me fifty quid a week. That's gone now. So, I'm paying this mortgage myself. And I'm working all week. I'm spending half my time scanning forms to send to housing benefit and sometimes I think they're just strolling around and they're on more than me. I'm telling you the world has gone mad. Those silent voters who voted the Tories in. Then they voted out of Europe. Everyone thought that was immigration. And has immigration changed? Has it fuck. That was all just to get Cameron out. You get all these brain-dead working-class people voting for the Tories. Makes them think they're middle class or something. They're deluded. And then you get these can't be bothered voting so we get what we end up with and then *they* start moaning about it.'

'Bad news.'

'Have I got time for a half? I'm getting a half. Look at this pub. Lovely place. Used to be a Temperance Hall. Then it was a snooker club. You see all those lights hanging down from the ceiling in rows? Well they used to be above the snooker tables. Anyway, finish your pint. We better get back. They'll all be waiting at the door. All queueing up like morons. That's why you never go back early at lunchtime. Oh, fatal that. Yeah, just go out the fire exit. You watch it, they'll be loads of them.'

Simon also lived in Didsbury. After work, we got on the tram together and went for another pint. I suggested the Metropolitan but he said he preferred the Railway. We went in and got a pint each and sat on stools near the window.

'What a day, eh? Like this boozer, nice place, they aren't all up their own arse like over the road. Cheapest pub in Didsbury too. Holts's house. Pint of Two Hoots for less than three quid. I like that Timmy Taylor's over the road but it's a bit dear and I got a bad hangover after last time I was in there.'

'Nice pint that.'

'Can you see them all going in? All those posh bastards. At least they get women over there. That's one thing you don't get in here, mate, and that's probably because of over the road. But I brought a bird in here and she liked it. There's little corners where you can get a bit of privacy.'

'Busy now.'

'Yeah. Rammed in here tonight. That bird I brought in here. She was from down south. I worked with her at Central. She wasn't sort of massively fit or anything but you know some women just have that effect on you. I only have to say her name to get a hard-on. You know what I mean? But she never liked me as much as I liked her. That time she came in here everyone started looking at me different though, like, how can he get a bird like that? Two-faced twats. That wore off anyway, since I haven't brought anyone else in since. Always go for a bird that likes you more than you like them, that's my advice.'

'Well, maybe.'

'Yeah, so, like I say, I'm on Clyde Road. You know what they say: everyone in Manchester has lived on Clyde Road at one time or another. Noisy neighbours I've got. Selfish bastards. Some people are just brain-dead. The landlord lives on the Wirral. Old bastard comes round, acts all frail and that, and you help him with ladders or something and then two months later the twat puts the rent up fifty quid. He knows I don't want to move again. Moving house, or flat in my case – nightmare. Every time I moved I was always well stressed and I wished I had all my books on Kindle instead of having to carry boxes and boxes. And I'm on the second floor in this place. I thought I was going to have a heart attack when I was moving in. I'm not moving again unless another bird turns up. The bloke who lives downstairs is called Peter O'Toole and he never makes a peep. I shit you not. I used to live next to a bloke called Vincent Van Gogh. No shit. You see post for people when you live in flats. I'm always signing for parcels and that. No fucker ever signs for one of mine though. I always have to go to the sorting office.'

'Ball ache.'

'That Lisa was so fit. But she drove me up the wall. Logically there was no reason to be with her. She wound me up to fuck. And she treated me like shit but I just kept going back. It was always me getting in touch with her first. You know what I mean? Sometimes she sent me pictures of her herself with fuck all on. I think she just liked the game. The thing was she didn't really like herself. She didn't like her tits. She said one was a bit smaller than the other. You really think that bothered me? But it bothered her. She didn't like her nipples either, said they were saggy. Again, can't say I noticed. She didn't like herself, like I say. She liked men to be arseholes. Well, she didn't like it, but that was the kind of man she always went for, she couldn't help it. I'm not an arsehole in that way. If I don't get enough kip I'm a grumpy fucker, don't get me wrong, but that's not the same, is it?'

'I know a woman like that.'

'Really?'

'Yep. She—'

'When I stand outside of here having a smoke I can see everything. You know what I mean? I can see the roof of the flats where I live, the barbers where I get my haircut, the estate agents, the tram stop, the roof of the flats where Lisa lives, the post office, the cash point, the curry house. Library is just a couple of tram stops away. Everything's on the doorstep. And this boozer where you can get a pint for less than three quid. Can't ask for much more than that.'

'Not bad this Two Hoots either.'

'I was listening to Spotify yesterday, you been on that? Bit of Teenage Fanclub. Never got round to them at the time. Love that guitar though. And obviously I'm not on the premium thing so you get all these adverts. There was this one to work in the Amazon warehouse and they said to look at happypacking.com and there was this giddy bird doing the voice-over and I thought, well it might be a change from the library. But then I looked into it and I'd have to get on the bus or the train to get there, so I thought I might as well just stay here. I applied to work at Aldi too.'

'Oh yeah?'

'Failed the online test. They give you a load of questions and situations with customers and that and I couldn't work out if they wanted you to sort things out yourself or go to the manager, so I thought I'll say go to the manager and anyway I failed it. Wasn't that arsed really. Only took me ten minutes and they're cheeky bastards at Aldi anyway. They don't even put a date on the veg.'

'Joke.'

'Where did you say you are living?'

'Old Lansdowne.'

'Have a told you about me landlord?'

'Yep.'

'Well, the letting agents are worse. I paid them this big fuck-off registration fee to pay for the bloke who sat on the couch and let me look around the flat, and what do I get out of them? Fuck all. Two hundred quid so they can email me a tenancy agreement? Robbing bastards them lot, I tell you. And the worst, you see the key-cutting place over there? Blaggs? I had to pay to get a key cut. You know when the guy comes from Npower or Eon or whatever? Well, all the meters where I live are in the cellar. And so you need the key for it. And I had to get it cut myself, four fucking quid. Cheeky bastards. Anyway, I'm getting another pint. Is there a band on tonight?

'Yeah.'

We got more beer in and listened to the music. Simon was having twice as many pints as me. And when the band finished he soon started talking again. People were always telling me about their lives. You shut the fuck up for long enough, they'll do that.

'Don't mind that Irish music, although that fiddle gets on your tits, dunnit? All my lot come from Portrush, round there. You been round there? Where that golfer's from? McIlroy? I remember once as a kid we went back for a holiday and me mum took me to see the seals. I couldn't see them on the rocks there, all camouflaged. But then she gave me the binoculars and I looked at them and they were all looking back at me. I shit you not. And I looked around at my mum and she pointed out some more. She was almost crying, and she said, "It's a grand soft day." I'll never forget that. It was like she was saying it to herself. Them seals were like, twisting and turning on the rocks, and then this big fucker came and he sort of swam like he was doing the butterfly, but with a massive splash every time. And I sat with me mum and we watched and she just smiled. Fuck's sake, getting all maudlin here. Get the violins out.'

'Nice phrase that.'

'What?'

'Grand soft day.'

'I know. But, you know, once, she broke her ribs and never told any fucker. She was that generation. Never told anyone about it for months. The old queen. I miss her. And it was the same at the end. By the time she told us it was all over anyway. Anyway, yeah, grand soft days. Are you having another? I know I am. Come on, you cunt, get it down your neck.'

I stayed for one more. I was on at Wythenshawe in the morning, opening up. I left Simon in there, chatting away to some other old fart, and walked the short distance back, past the fancy restaurants on Lapwing Lane. On Old Lansdowne, the branches of tall trees covered the streetlights, and there was a fox, darting across the road.

My head was still pounding as I got off the 43 in the morning. I dragged myself up to the staff room. Kerry looked a bit hungover too. I asked about her kid and she said he was fine though her husband was a dickhead, even if she loved him. I had a wash in the bathroom and then got the keys off one of the managers.

As I approached the glass doors with the keys I could see a bearded old man in a wheelchair. Behind the wheelchair were a number of bobbing heads, craning necks and eyes squinting through the glass. I unlocked the door and waved them all in. Some went upstairs to get on computers, while others headed straight for the counter.

'I'll have *The Times* please,' said the man in the wheelchair to Kerry.

'Ah, good morning. Card. No card,' said an Asian man to me.

'I'm sorry?'

'No card.'

'You don't have your card?'

'No, my name is Mu—'

'Your name. Block capitals,' I said, passing the man a sheet of scrap paper and a pen. It was what Colin did.

'Who's next?' I said, beckoning over the next person in the queue, a man with a Polish accent.

'I've lost my—'

'Block capitals, on here.'

Both Kerry and I were busy dealing with enquiries when a big man with a tattoo of a spider on his right cheek came up to the counter. 'Got to send a fax. Which one of you can send a fax? Where do I send a fax?'

'I won't be a moment, sir. Please join the queue,' said Kerry.

'I need to send a fax now,' said the man.

'Upstairs,' I said, pointing.

'How do I get upstairs?'

'Stairs on your left. Lift down there.'

'I'm not going in no lift. Where's the stairs, mate?'

'On your left,' I said, pointing, before returning to the customer on the counter, a young woman with a baby in a pram. I wrote out her library number so she could log on to a computer. Within minutes she'd come back.

'It says I'm suspended. Why's that?'

'There might be an issue on the card.'

'What issue? I haven't been in for ages.'

'Give me that scrap of paper with your number on, please.'

I looked her up on the system. 'It says you have eighteen pounds in fines.'

'Eighteen pound? Since when?'

'Some have been on a while.'

'I'm not paying no fine. I haven't been in here for years. I've never heard of those books.'

'I haven't told you what the books are yet.'

'Are you being funny, mate?'

'I'm just telling you what's on the screen.'

'Well I don't have no eighteen pound in fines. Something wrong there. Can't you change it?'

'I have to do what's on the screen.'

'You're having a laugh, mate. I'll use another library then. Fuck this.'

'There's no need for that.'

'No need? You're a wanker, mate. All I wanted to do was print off a job application and now I can't.'

'There's no need for that language.'

'Nah, there is. You're a wanker,' she said, on her way out with the pram.

'Who's next, please?'

'Hiya,' she said, putting some children's books on the counter. She was another local woman, a regular.

'Are you returning these or taking them out?'

'Returning.'

'Okay,' I said, scanning the books. 'Thank you.'

'Thanks, love.'

'Is it break time yet?' I said, looking across at Kerry.

An elderly woman came in. She returned eight books from a shopping cart. Half an hour later she came back with eight romance novels to take out. I looked at her borrower record and saw that she'd had over a thousand loans.

At break time, I took my usual seat at the table and drank my tea while reading through the *Manchester Evening News* from back to front.

'Nice morning,' said Kerry, looking out of the window.

When she sat down, Kerry looked across at me and smiled. She had a sip of tea and then looked at her phone. 'You not on Facebook?'

'What?' I said, looking up but still turning a page in the paper. 'Facebook? Yeah, sometimes.'

'What about the eBooks? Have you downloaded the app?'

'I like proper books.'

'But we've had the training.'

'Training to make ourselves redundant. Great.'

'Don't be daft. You won't get redundancy anyway.'

'Prefer books. And proper newspapers.'

I stared out of the window. It was raining on the betting shops and discount stores of the Civic Centre. A thin man stood drinking a can of Foster's. A grey-haired woman pushed a pram outside Wilko. A tram headed for Manchester Airport with a couple of stewardesses on board dressed in bright red uniforms.

'You're on ref, next. Bit of a break for you,' said Kerry.

'Oh, Kerry, *why* did you say that? Never say that.'

'Ha. That's what Colin says.'

After break, I made the short walk over to the reference desk. I logged on to the staff computer, and had a look at the reservations. I clicked on the coloured blocks to check the names. Three of the usuals: Mark, David and Geoffrey C. Geoffrey C would no doubt be over in a minute to ask something about the internet. David was watching an episode of a crime series set in Scandinavia. At the other computers, there were two young lads. They stank of weed and were playing computer games.

I gazed out of the window again. There were grey skies over the station interchange. Like Colin had said, the library wasn't the same any more. It used to be full of books. And it used to be quiet. Now it was full of kids all the time and you spent half the day printing stuff out for people or helping them fill out benefit forms. We weren't even called library assistants. We were 'Neighbourhood Delivery Assistants' or 'NDAs'.

'Excuse me, mate. Sent some printing,' said a young lad who'd approached the counter.

'Okay,' I said, checking the screen. 'what computer are you on?'

'Er . . . five.'

'Fifteen pages?'

'Something like that.'

'That will be three pounds, please.'

I put the money in the till and then walked over to the printer. When the last of the fifteen pages printed off, I passed the sheets to the young man, who began looking through them.

'These aren't what I printed.'

'Sorry?'

'These are wrong, mate.'

'We can only print out what you send.'

'I know but these aren't right. There's some missing and then some are done twice. Your printer has printed the wrong ones off.'

'Whatever you sent to the printer is what you've got there.'

'That's bullshit.'

'What can I say?'

'Can you do it again?'

'You'll have to send it again.'

'But I've run out of time.'

'You can get another hour for £1.50.'

'I've already give you three quid for fuck all.'

'First hour is free.'

'That's bullshit, mate,' he said, walking off. 'You're a tosser.'

'No need for that.'

'Tosser.'

When the man had left, another man on a computer, Mark, piped up: 'You're out of order there, mate.'

'Why am I out of order?'

'This library is a joke. It's the worst one around. The staff are awful.'

'I can only print off what people send.'

'Come on, mate, you could have helped him a bit more.'

'He called me a tosser.'

'Well, I agree that's out of order. But this library, mate. The library service is not what it was.'

'At least it's free.'

'Ah, but no, it is not, is it? We pay taxes. It's our taxes that pay for these libraries.'

'But you're on the dole, aren't you?'

'Ah, you think you're being funny there, but you're not. I've paid loads of taxes.'

'I know but you aren't paying any now.'

'You see? This is what I'm talking about,' he said, looking around.

'They are very helpful, I find,' said Geoffrey C.

'To you, maybe. Depends who you get. Some staff here they will let you off with a bit of printing. Or they'll let you have a bit of extra on the computer. He won't,' he said, gesturing towards me.

'I just stick to the rules,' I said.

'Come on, mate, play the white man.'

'You can't win with some people.'

'It's your attitude, mate.'

'I'm doing my best.'

After Mark left, I looked up his record on the system. He'd taken loads of DVDs out, mainly vampire films and chick flicks, and fine after fine had been waived on his behalf.

At lunchtime, I walked across the road to The Silver Birch, got a pint of lager and took it outside into the beer garden. The sun was out and I watched the aeroplanes. It was five-past before I headed back.

I looked at the timetable in the empty staff room and then put a piece of chewing gum in my mouth. I was on the reference desk again. I sat there looking at the BBC Sport website. I watched Ronnie O'Sullivan make another 147. Then a woman came up. I paused the snooker.

'You do the faxes?'

'Er . . . yes, I do.'

'Where is it? How much is it? I need to send all these sheets to my solicitor. How much does it cost?'

'Just here,' I said, walking over to the fax machine.

'This is what I need to send,' she said, holding out three bits of paper.

'It's one pound fifty for the first sheet and a pound a sheet after that.'

'So how much?'

'Three pound fifty.'

'Three pound fifty,' she said, reaching into her purse. She dropped three pound coins on the counter, then a pile of change from which she fished out the remaining fifty pence made up of five pees and coppers.

'What's the fax number?'

'I'm not exactly sure. Can I use your phone a minute?'

'Well—'

She picked up the phone before I could answer. 'Won't be a minute, love, I just need to get this fax number. Got no credit on the moby . . . Hiya Darryl, I need the fax number for the solicitor . . . yeah . . . do you know it . . . well can you find it for me . . . I'm in the library . . . I need to send this fax . . . they need to know it! Just find me the number!'

I waited patiently. 'Sorry, love, won't be a minute' she said, looking in my direction but not making eye contact. 'Excuse me, love, have you got a pen and paper I can lend?' she said. 'Thanks, love . . . Okay, give me the number. Slow down! Okay that's it,' she said, putting the phone down.

Downstairs, I stood at the counter ripping the first page out of books again, and then deleting the books on the system. A woman turned up on a mobility scooter. Her borrower record showed she was born in 1921. She looked at the reservation shelf, reached up to take a book off it and then reversed the scooter. It beeped as she reversed. Lights flashed. She parked the scooter near the iMac computer then stood up and took a tablet out of the basket on the front of her scooter and walked very slowly over to me, passing me her reservation, a novel by Nora Roberts called *Night Shift*.

'Excuse me, love, when you have done that can you help me? You have always been very helpful before,' she said, putting a tablet on the desk. I'd never seen her.

'I will do my best. I'm not really the expert on these things,' I said.

'It is just that I can't send this email to my granddaughter. It won't send. This is the address,' she said, passing me a notebook.

'So, this is where you want to send it?'

'Yes. And I don't want to lose what I have already written down.'

'Okay, let me have a look.'

'Thank you very much. I'm very thankful.'

'A pleasure, Mrs Wall.'

'We're going to Chester Races again.'

'Oh yes? Will you be having a bet?'

'Oh yes, love. Otherwise what would be the point?'

'I'm not a gambler myself.'

'Oh, there's no harm in it, love.'

'Ah, I can see what has happened. You see the email address here?' I said, pointing to the screen. 'You've put a full stop at the end. You see? You've put a full stop at the end of the email. So, I've deleted that. You never do that.'

'I can't see that. You haven't deleted the email, have you?'

'No, no . . . just the full stop.'

'Oh, thank you so much. I couldn't bear to write all that again.'

'There you go. It has been sent now.'

'Are you sure, love?'

'Yes, look. You see this folder. Where it says 'Sent'. You can see it there.'

'Oh, just let me write that down,' she said, writing the date and time in her notebook.

After afternoon break, a young man came up to me and spoke in a whisper. He had a bushy beard and a slicked back hipster haircut.

'Hi, hi, can I have a word with you? It is a sensitive topic but I need to change my name on my library card.'

'Oh yes?'

'The thing is,' he said, 'I . . . I . . . was recently mugged.'

He looked a bit upset so I just changed the name on the system, and didn't charge him for the new card. It saved arguing.

'Thank you very much, sir,' said the man, before walking out of the library.

'You fell for that one,' said Kerry.

'What do you mean?'

'He's always getting new cards. What was the reason this time?'

'He said he'd been mugged.'

'He's used that one before.'

'Really? Why didn't you tell me?'

'You can't really. Not when they're stood there. He might put a complaint in.'

'God, I'm such a mug.'

'Don't worry about it.'

'Anyway, what does being mugged have to do with a library card?'

'Exactly. I'm surprised you haven't seen him before. But I guess if you haven't you wouldn't know. I've done at least two for him.'

'You know, sometimes I give up. I got mugged once. With a knife. Wasn't a joke.'

'No, no. You did the right thing really. Just give them what they want. Avoids the hassle.'

The computers went off at quarter to five. At ten-to, I flicked the lights on and off as Kerry walked around the library to see if anyone was still in. The dates on the stamps were changed, and we'd already cashed up and brought our bags and coats down, ready to leave. Just then a man walked in wearing a dark blue suit.

'We close in five minutes,' I said. 'It's almost five now, I need to lock up.'

'But it isn't five.'

'By the time everyone gets out and I lock the door it will be.'

'It isn't five yet.'

'Look, mate, can't you understand that we just want to go home?'

'It isn't five.'

'We've been open since nine this morning.'

'But what about my printing?'

'We open again at nine in the morning.'

'Is there anywhere else?'

'No,' I said, picking up the keys. 'We are open tomorrow. And Monday and Tuesday we are open until eight.'

'You don't have to shake your keys, mate.'

I beckoned him towards the door.

'Don't wave your arms, either.'

'We're closing now. Open again at nine, tomorrow. You got your stuff, Kerry? Okay, come on, mate, out we go.'

The man walked off towards the car park as Kerry waited for me to lock the door. Again, I waited ages for the bus. When it arrived, it was packed out with people coming back from the airport.

The next morning, after stamping the newspapers, I was at the counter when the young man with the hipster haircut and bushy beard turned up again.

'Did you give me that new card last night? I don't remember taking it with me.'

'I gave it to you.'

'Are you sure? I don't remember taking it. Are you sure you gave it to me? Has anyone handed it in?'

'You took it. I saw you take it.'

'What's with the attitude?'

'It is not an attitude. I gave you the new card last night. And I believe it isn't the first time you've had a new card. What's your name again?'

'Excuse me?'

'You've had new cards before.'

'Why are you trying to intimidate me?'

'Intimidate you? I'm perfectly calm. I just don't like being made a mug of. Now if you tell me your name I can see if it has been handed in.'

'I don't like your attitude and you shouldn't speak to me like that. I'd like to talk to a manager please.'

'Not a problem.'

A few minutes later two of the managers came down. As I waited by the counter, they walked with the young man to the other side of the library and listened as he gave his version of events. Then they came back to the counter with the man, and he said, 'After talking to your manager, I'm prepared to give you the chance to apologise.'

'I'm not apologising.'

'I'm giving you the chance to apologise. If you apologise to me now I won't put in a formal complaint.'

'Apologise? What for? I only gave you a new card last night. And now you want another one.'

'You said I've had *loads of cards.* You said *allegedly* I've already had *loads of new cards.* I've had *four* new cards. That's not loads.'

'I didn't use the word "allegedly".'

'Oh my god, you did.'

'That's not a word I would use.'

'Oh my god. Are you going to apologise?'

'No.'

'*Are* you going to apologise?'

'No.'

'You've said that *allegedly* I've had loads of cards already.

And when I asked you if a card had been handed in you didn't look.'

'I asked you for your name.'

'No, you didn't.'

'I can't look for a lost card without a name.'

'*Are* you going to apologise?'

'You keep changing what I said.'

'*Are* you going to apologise?'

'No. I'm not. You're an arsehole.'

There was a gasp from the managers. I was told by one of them to go upstairs to the staff room. I waited and waited. At lunchtime, I went out to the Silver Birch and had a pint, watched the aeroplanes again. After the pint, I decided to just go home. I walked through the industrial estate at Sharston, and then at Boat Lane in Northenden I passed the old Tatton Arms and walked down the river, enjoying the sunshine. People were walking their dogs at leisure. One big old black Labrador bounded along as best he could and went crashing into the water, and the water splashed everywhere. I carried on walking, under the motorway bridge and on down the towpath, the noise of the cars replaced by the gentle swish of golf clubs. A couple of buzzards played together in the sky.

My spirits lifted, I carried on walking beyond Didsbury. At Chorlton Water Park I sat on a bench and watched the geese flying low across the length of the lake. They looked so clumsy on land, arguing over the food tossed to them, but in flight they were majestic.

I sat on a bench and thought of Zlata. I gave her a call. 'They are probably going to sack me from this library job I've been doing,' I said.

'Why?'

'I called someone an arsehole.'

She laughed. 'Well that's great. Very good. Well done, Mr Writer. That was good job. Another good job. What are you going to live on now? Poems?'

'I have a few hundred quid in the bank.'

'That's nothing.'

'Gives me breathing space.'

'But what are you going to do?'

'Maybe they won't sack me. It's pretty hard to get sacked these days.'

'Not when you are not permanent.'

'How have you been, anyway?'

'I have been looking after Luka.'

'I want to see you.'

'Why?'

'I miss you.'

'I miss you too.'

'Okay if I come to yours?'

'Okay, but I need to get dressed.'

'It will take me about half an hour.'

'Okay.'

I crossed the bridge over the river, took the road through the woods and came out near the Lebanese restaurant in Northern Moor. I crossed Sale Road and headed for Button Lane. When Zlata let me in I saw she was still in a dressing gown.

'Thought you were getting dressed?' I said.

'No point,' she said. 'Let's go upstairs.'

She closed the curtains and we got into bed. I shoved the cuddly toys out of the way. I kissed her breasts and she froze. Then she moved away and we lay at either side of the bed, a gap between us.

'I want you to hurt me,' she said.

'What?'

'I want you to hurt me.'

She pulled back the covers and then lay on her front.

'I want you to hit me.'

I spanked her arse.

'Harder,' she said.

I did it harder.

'Harder,' she said. 'I want you to hurt me.'

Her arse cheeks were red from the slapping but still it wasn't hard enough for her. I felt stupid.

'Forget it,' she said.

In the morning, she was still sleeping, and I thought about Platt Fields. The cold winter sun mixing the light. The sound of buses on Yew Tree Lane. Further away, the buses on Oxford Road, the old Finglands ones, orange trimmed, pulling into the depot there to change drivers. Near where Hardy's Well used to be, with its white wall overlooking the beer garden, a white wall with the black words of the Manchester poet Lemn Sissay, every word beginning with a W, a poem to lift your heart if you were on that bus, a poem now reduced to rubble, even in memory. And there were the old brick buildings still standing across the road in the park. The tended gardens. Crows in the tall trees of the park, calling out to each other. Ducks across the pond, parts of which were frozen. The kids' play area near the pond. The little iron fence around the rim of the pond. Mums and Dads pushing prams in the park, wheels wobbling across the concrete. Dog walkers, and their dogs padding across the grass, leaving paw prints on the frost. And beyond them, at the very far end of the park, at the corner of Platt Lane and Yew Tree Lane, there, within shouting distance of Maine Road itself, the old-style AstroTurf pitch of the training ground, slick and hard with a shimmering of ice, and a young man, for whom it is already too late, trying to come back, carrying a leg that feels heavier than the other, his mind still telling him to do what he can no longer do, and he comes off the pitch and the other lads aren't so friendly, he feels that something has changed in them, something has gone from them, not him, but he doesn't know that yet, and can't put his finger on it, and the buses keep passing and the crows keep calling.

On the Monday, I'd not heard anything from the library, so just went in as though nothing had happened. I could see that people were surprised to see me and were tiptoeing around, but not Colin.

'Well, you have put your foot in it there,' he said.

'I guess so.'

'Management will get you in.'

'Shit happens.'

'It does. You are right. Listen, you want my advice?'

'Okay.'

'Say you've been having problems at home or something. Some problem in your personal life.'

'I don't need excuses.'

'Just take it from me. I've been around a long time. I know what they are like.'

It was late morning when I was told to go up to the staff room and wait again. I sat in there for the best part of an hour, and then I was told that I would be meeting Nigel, the manager from Central, the top man. I was to go to meeting room 2.

I went in there and Nigel was waiting. He stood up and smiled. There was barely room for the table and two chairs.

'Come in,' he said, 'sit down. Now, you obviously know why you are in here.'

'Think so,' I said, the smile on his face making me think I might be fine.

'You realise that language like that is unacceptable.'

'Well, it was what led up to it really. The bloke was trying to get a new card and—'

'People can be difficult. In libraries. It is part of the job. Your behaviour was unacceptable,' he said. The smile had gone.

'Don't I get to give you my version? What about my side?'

'It doesn't matter. What you said is unacceptable.'

'I know but there are reasons.'

'What you said . . . we can't have that.'

'Seems a bit harsh.'

'If you were permanent staff I'd have to put you on suspension. But the contract you are on . . . the truth is we could have let you go at any time. And this isn't the only thing that has been brought up.'

'What else has been said?'

'It doesn't matter now.'

'Don't I get to give you my side?'

'What you said is unacceptable. We can't have staff talking to the public like that.'

'But I was provoked.'

'That is neither here nor there.'

'Thing is, I've been having problems at home.'

'Well, I'm sorry to hear that.'

'It might have affected me, I don't know.'

'Like I say, I'm sorry to hear that.'

'This seems so harsh.'

'I have no alternative.'

'Course you have. You could let me off.'

'You give me no alternative.'

'We could put it down to experience.'

'I'm afraid it was unacceptable. You give me no alternative.'

'Well, I'm not going to beg you,' I said, before getting up and walking out of there. He followed me into the staff room, where I got my coat. The two managers were in there, the two who'd reported what I'd said. They avoided eye contact, looked at their computer screens.

'Keep looking out for number one,' I said to them, on the way out. There was no reply.

I went downstairs and down to the counter, where I gave Colin my name tag.

'Been good working with you,' I said.

'So, they have let you go? For that?'

'Yep.'

'That's out of order.'

'It's because I'm not permanent. I've got no rights.'

'So that's it?'

'Yep.'

'Well, I'm sorry.'

'Don't worry. It's my own fault. I'll be fine. I'll find something else. Thanks for your advice anyway. I might come in and see you some time.'

'This is all wrong,' he said.

I phoned Zlata about it when I got home, and she invited me round for something to eat. I couldn't afford the tram so I got the 41 to Sale Road and walked down Button Lane. Zlata let me in, then we walked into the kitchen where the washing machine was on.

'Why is that always going?' I said.

'It is a shared house. Always washing machine and banging doors. It is a miracle Luka sleeps.'

'How's the food going?' I asked.

'Has been a disaster.'

'Oh.'

'I put too much salt in, then tried to recover with lemon, but now it tastes awful.'

'Smells good to me.'

'I don't think we should try it. Let's go to take away.'

'I'm not going there again. That curry and chips was awful.'

'It is a Caribbean place.'

'I know.'

'I told you the gravy would be different.'

'Let's just have this, you've spent all this time cooking.'

'Okay, you go and sit in the living room. I will check on the baby then continue cooking.'

I saw the baby monitor, heard Zlata speaking gently. I looked out past the rowing machine and through the patio doors. There was frost on the grass. Tall trees beyond the houses opposite were outlined against a pink sky. Crows called, and I heard geese flying over.

'Okay, here we are,' said Zlata, passing me the plate.

'What are we calling this?'

'Cauliflower curry, with chick peas.'

'Okay then.'

I had as much as I could take. Zlata ate all of hers.

'You didn't finish.'

'No. I tried my best. I didn't like it.'

'Okay.'

'I will wash up.'

'You don't have to.'

'It's fine.'

I was still washing up after she'd checked on Luka. She seemed to have used every pot in the kitchen. I heard her padding across the kitchen floor in her slippers. She pressed against me, her chest on my back. I dried my hands on the pot towel and we went upstairs.

She had to have the lights off now. In the darkness, I struggled to find my way. We tried different positions. She froze again. I needed to put the light on but she said no. I wanted to see her. She went down on me but used her tongue too much and it tickled.

At breakfast, she said I would have to get a good job or else there was no point in us being together. I decided to walk home to save money. I knew it wasn't happening with Zlata. For a time, I thought if we got to know each other better, things would improve, but she never seemed to take my side and I always felt pissed off after seeing her.

I was still pissed off about the library job too. It was easy. Paid the rent and gave me time to write. But maybe I was better off out of Manchester libraries. After all, they were the people who had got rid of a load of books without asking anyone.

It was obvious I wouldn't be able to get a job in another Manchester library. But a temporary job came up at one in Tameside and they invited me for an interview. I thought about what Zlata had said as I got on the 169 and headed for Ashton.

First, they gave me some old library cards with authors'

names on that I had to put in alphabetical order within five minutes. Then two women asked me five questions each about what I would do to help the future of the library. At the end, they asked me if I had any questions. I asked them how 'temporary' the job would be. They said two months. They wanted someone to tide them over until the self-service machines were installed. They were interviewing all week. They had had a 'phenomenal response' for this temporary, eighteen-hours-per-week post.

The library in Ashton was like a mausoleum. The town was twenty years behind central Manchester. In Ashton town centre, the amusements arcade next to the old Metro cinema was still there, but the cinema was long gone, having lost out to the multiplex on the edge of town. The greasy spoon café was still there. The precinct centre was filled with vape shops and the smell of piss. Old people trudged up and down. Mobility scooters were all over. It was like death. The place of my birth felt like death to me. What had happened to it? Hundreds of us were scrabbling for some crap job in a desolate library. And meanwhile, half the land they sold on Ashton Moss was still left as wasteland, no longer even green. The burger places and the cinema and the bowling alley on the outskirts of town were there for you if you had a car, but as I sat on the 216 heading out of Ashton towards Droylsden, I didn't recognise anything until I reached the Snipe pub, still standing and done up, and Topps Tiles, still there. I passed Ryecroft Hall in Audenshaw, where I'd used the library as a boy, and the blinds were down on the windows.

The bus carried on to the windswept crossroads at Droylsden. The old Cotton Tree pub where a gangster had shot someone had been turned into a garish Indian restaurant, and the Concord Suite was a shadow of its old self, and the Marina, so-called, was still being fashioned on the canal, and as the bus carried on down Ashton New Road, we passed the Jolly Carter pub and Cemetery Road and the old funeral homes, and, beyond Edge Lane, we headed on down to the glorious complex of the Etihad Stadium, with the training pitches and the bridge across the road, and the stadium in which they trained. I thought back to the old days on Platt Lane again, when anyone could watch the training session of the first team, and I thought of those old facilities, that rock-hard AstroTurf pitch, and my heart broke, my heart broke for Ashton and Droylsden, and my heart broke for myself, because even if I hadn't got injured I'd have been playing in the wrong era. That Marcus Rashford was on thousands a week, good luck to him, he was good. But players with half my talent were now millionaires, and I didn't feel reasonable or philosophical about that. I had been sitting in a room with two corpses for women asking me daft questions about a library and a job that meant fuck all to me, and if my answers showed I didn't give a shit I couldn't help it. I just didn't know how I was going to come to terms with all of life just seeming crap, an anti-climax, a lifetime of living 'after the Lord Mayor's show'. I still didn't know what it was I could do to be happy except describe some of the world as I saw it in the best way I could, filling notebooks into the night as a way to stay alive.

On the following Wednesday, Dave and Linda agreed to look after Luka while me and Zlata went to the poetry night at Fuel. Zlata didn't seem interested, but I had a few beers with Ron and enjoyed myself. At the end of the night me and Zlata walked across the road to the bus stop, where there were half a dozen other people waiting for the 41 to Sale. Zlata had also had a few pints and I had to hold her hand so she could cross the road safely.

'What did you think?' I asked her.

'The poetry?'

'Yes, well, the night as a whole.'

'Well, you ignored me.'

'Didn't mean to.'

'Well, you did. You ask about the poetry. I have to say that the poetry in my country is better. My country is better for everything. The food is better.'

I heard a muttering from the bus queue.

'There were some good readers.'

'Yes, some performers were good. But the poetry was not like the poetry in my country. Maybe it is because we had war, but the young poets in my country are so sensitive, so profound, so political.'

'You can't say there wasn't any political poetry.'

'Oh yes. Your friend Ron. Very political. I liked him. But it is so much better in my country. My country has more soul than here. Here there is no soul. And the weather is awful in this country. Always raining.'

'Go home then,' said a bloke in the queue.

'No need for that, mate,' I said, turning around.

'I'm not talking to you,' he said. 'I'm talking to her. Your bird.'

'Oh, come on, mate,' I said.

'What do you mean "come on"? What you going to do about it?'

'Don't be an arsehole,' I said.

'I'm talking to your skanky bitch,' he said, pointing at Zlata. 'Why don't you fuck off back to Poland? Stop taking our jobs, coming over here and sending all your money back home.'

'Ha! I am not from Poland!' said Zlata.

'Fuck off back to Poland.'

The bus finally turned up. We got on first and went upstairs. But the bloke followed us up there and sat on the seat behind.

'Do you have to sit there?' I asked him.

'What are you going to do about it? Nothing, right? We know that. Don't you have anything to say, love? Can you understand me?'

'I understand perfect.'

'I used to have a house, and a building job, and now because of all you immigrants coming in I don't have a job or a house and I've lost my family.'

'That is not my fault.'

'Look around you. When I'm on this bus there's no English on it. The driver is not even English. You tell him where you're getting off and he's no idea of the names of any of the roads. And it's you Polish are the worst.'

'I'm *not* Polish.'

'What do you have to say, mate? This your girlfriend or not? What's wrong, couldn't find an English bird?'

'Shall we go downstairs?' I said to Zlata, holding her hand. She shook my hand off, but followed me.

'He will just come down to us,' she said, joining me at the back of the bus.

'We will see.'

'You didn't stand up for me.'

'I don't know anything about politics.'

'You are weak. And your writing is shit.'

'Oh, don't start with that again,' I said.

'You are weak. This is your fault.'

'How is this my fault?'

'It has been awful tonight.'

'He's just pissed. And look, he's not coming down.'

'You didn't say anything.'

'What can you say?'

'I think you should not come to my house.'

'Oh, come on. I'm sorry.'

'You didn't stand up for me. And you ignored me in the pub.'

'I told you, I'm not into politics.'

'You didn't say anything. Get off the bus.'

'What?'

'Get off the bus here. We are in Didsbury.'

'I'm not getting off. I'm coming to yours.'

We sat there in silence as the bus made its way down Palatine Road, above the moonlit Mersey, below the M60. The bus went through Northenden, with all its restaurants and takeaways, Indian, Chinese, Vietnamese, Thai. The man upstairs got off near a Polish grocery, and gave us a V-sign through the window. And then there were the pubs and bars with people stood smoking outside. We passed the Britannia Airport Hotel, where, according to Zlata, there were a load of asylum seekers staying, waiting to be housed, and took a right turn near Wythenshawe Park, up through Moor Village before we got off the bus. We passed the Caribbean takeaway and walked towards Zlata's. Still she said nothing. We went in through the little wooden gate. She took her keys out and opened the door. As she walked inside I began to follow her but she started closing the door on me.

'Oh, come on, don't be silly.'

'Go away,' she said. 'Go away! Leave me alone!'

As the door slammed shut I just stood there. I looked at the bell, then I turned and walked away. I headed for the bus stop on Sale Road. I looked at the timetable and realised there were no more buses. I started walking back. A fox darted across the road. In Moor Village, near the post office, there were a load of wheelie bins and rubbish bags. Next to them was an old football. At first, I thought I'd kick it all the way home, but when I got through Northenden, and went under the motorway, my knee was killing me, so I chipped the ball over the bridge and down into the Mersey, where it landed with a splash before floating away.

At home, I picked up my notebook and opened it to the next blank page, where I jotted down an idea I'd had for a short story. Looking across at the desk, I saw piles of old notebooks. I looked back at the new idea in the notebook, then put it next to the computer before going to bed.

I wrote the first draft of the short story in the morning and then in the afternoon saw a message on Facebook from Ron. He'd had a skip delivered to his house by the council and wanted some help clearing up.

I got on the 43 and headed for Wythenshawe. We went through the station interchange and passed the library. We carried on towards the airport and then the bus dropped me off in the place Ron had described, opposite Palatable Pizza. There was a convenience store and a few other shops in the tiny precinct centre. I walked through that and then through a rough estate of flimsy-looking houses where the front doors led straight out onto the street.

Ron opened the door to the tiny house, his huge frame filling the doorway. I walked in through a hallway cluttered with old coats and books and into the living room, where I saw the cheery face of Bill, another of the poets from Fuel. They had already done a bit of work and were having a rest. Soon it was time to start again.

We started in the back bedroom, where Ron had to forcibly shove open the door because of the piles of junk inside. First, we smashed up an old bed frame and carted the bits outside to the skip. Then, armed with a thick roll of bin bags we each took turns to fill one. I found a Doc Martens shoe, size seven and a half. Ron said to throw any of those out. I counted five in total, dragged out from the rubbish. There were old rucksacks, TVs, computer monitors, computer magazines. Ron stopped a moment and showed me the box his dad's catheters had come in.

'He had to insert that in himself and then feed it through all the way through his body,' said Ron. 'It's about two feet long.'

There were several of these long blue boxes. 'Looks grim,' I said.

'Comes to us all.'

'Cheers.'

'I'm not joking. People roll along, day after day and they haven't got a clue what's coming. Make the most of your time, I'm telling you. People don't realise what happens when you get old. I looked after my parents for years here but people don't know what I had to do really. You see how tiny this house is? Three people, two of them disabled. Can you imagine? I saved the government thousands in care home fees and all they did was take my benefits away when my mum and dad died.

A week later. Things can change overnight, I tell you. People don't realise that someday they might need someone to wipe their arse for them. And what if there's nobody there to do it?'

We carried on tidying up. There were old trainers. A football that went into the crowd at Maine Road while Ron was there, or so he said, a football that he shoved up his jumper and kept. It was a Mitre one, with arrows on, a luminous one too, that they used to use when it snowed. He was keeping that. He found some old pictures of his parents and kept them too. There were poetry books, mostly by William Blake. There was copy after copy of issue 1 of a magazine he'd once edited. There were rarer finds of issues 2 and 3, and he kept those. There were tins of beans and soup all over the floor, and he stacked these up on the windowsill. There was a broken ironing board, box after empty cardboard box, torn old coats, faded towels, random socks, a broken iron, a bottle of port, cans of Guinness Original, a pair of dusty binoculars, notebooks filled with poems. There were two Zimmer frames, and books, piles of books. Some he gave to me: a biography of Jim Morrison, a book called *70 Walks in Arran*, poetry by Boris Pasternak, stories by Kafka called *Wedding Preparations in the Country and Other Stories*, a Burroughs and Kerouac book called *And the Hippos Were Boiled in Their Tanks*, and another biography, *The Voice is All: The Lonely Victory of Jack Kerouac*.

We trailed up and down the stairs, made even narrower by the stair-lift that was still there but that the council had switched off. Outside it was pissing down. Before the airport, it had been rural round there. Ron told me about the fields and birds. Soon the skip began to fill up. The two Zimmer frames were a sad sight but Ron said neither had been of use.

Ron's knee was giving him some pain, and so was mine. There were old-fashioned knee braces among the junk, and, I never realised, but Ron told me he'd been a footballer too. He said when he got injured his dad had carried him off the pitch. There were oil paintings all over the place, painted by Ron's dad. Usually coastal scenes, where the sea was painted expertly, and the paintings were always signed with two little birds in the top right-hand corner. Ron saved all those, eventually putting them up on the walls.

On the way up and down the stairs I kept glancing in at the front bedroom. Ron saw me looking.

'I know what you're thinking, but I can't kip in there,' he said. 'They both died in there. I watched both my parents die in that bed. That's why I just kip downstairs.'

'Fair enough.'

'People don't like to talk about death. We hide it away. I can see now, you're uncomfortable talking about it. But other countries aren't like that. In Mexico, they celebrate the dead. Here we hide it away with polite phrases. People die around us all the time but we never see it.'

We carried on working, up and down the stairs, bin bag after bin bag filled with things no longer wanted. And then it was finally there. The carpet. We had reached down through the junk and found the light blue carpet. We made a pathway to the far corner of the room. Ron said he hadn't been able to reach that part of the room for ten years. He was now able to reach the window and open it. A plane roared overhead.

In the living room, there were piles of books on the chairs, and now the back room had been partly cleared there was room for some of them up there. The Kerouac books on the windowsill had been bloated by dripping rain that had come down from peeled-away paper on the ceiling. Ron gave me his rain-damaged copy of *Visions of Cody*. I looked out at the rain. It felt cosy in the living room, what with all the books lining the walls and the little gas fire on.

I kept looking through the window. In the garden, there was an old wheelchair folded up and rusting, leaning under the cover of an arbour. I sipped from the Arran whisky Ron had poured, and listened to the rain on the window.

As he made a Thai curry in the tiny kitchen, me and Bill looked through the books Ron had given us. Bill had got some Geoffrey Hill poems and BS Johnson stories. As well as the books, Ron had given me an old City programme, one from a game with AC Milan at Maine Road back in 1978. Bill poured red wine into a large pink goblet and I sipped more of my Arran whisky.

After the curry, Ron sat there going on and on about all the books and films he'd seen recently. Bill cheered up even more, as he always did when wine and poetry were involved. We watched DVDs of *Big Sur*, *On the Road* and *Howl*. In a scene from *Howl* there was Kerouac, Ginsberg and Burroughs in discussion. At that moment, I turned and looked at the three of us, and something about it made me glad.

# *Acknowledgements*

THANKS AGAIN TO Chris, Jen and Nick at Salt. And to John G Hall for the inspiration. Naomi, the next one is for you.